Your body was made for a lover's touch....

Lynne stiffened, stopped brushing her hair in midstroke and stared wide-eyed into the large oval mirror. Those words had come to her from a memory—she *remembered* Jarrett breathing the words against her neck, yet he had never said anything of the kind.

Suddenly the mirror clouded with a misty vapor, and a diffusion of light narrowed her vision. Like someone disappearing into a fog, her reflected figure blurred and faded. Dizziness made her put a hand on the tall frame for support.

She looked back into the mirror. No longer was she wearing her high-necked flannel nightgown. Her body was draped in a seductive, creamy satin gown, and Jarrett suddenly stood behind her, slipping the thin straps from her shoulders.

She turned to face him and held out her arms—yet no one was there....

Dear Reader,

This month we welcome you to a new venture from Silhouette Books—Shadows, a line designed to send shivers up your spine and chill you even while it thrills you. These are romances, but romances with a difference. That difference is in the fear you'll feel as you journey with the heroine to the dark side of love . . . then emerge triumphantly into the light. Who *is* the Shadows hero? Is he on the side of the angels? Sometimes. But sometimes neither you nor the heroine can be sure and you wonder, *Does he want to kiss me—or kill me?*

And what a lineup of authors we have for you. This month we're bringing you *four* tantalizing, terrifying titles by authors you won't be able to resist. Heather Graham Pozzessere is known to romance readers everywhere, but in *The Last Cavalier* she demonstrates an ability to spook you that will . . . well . . . haunt you long after you've turned the last page. In *Who Is Deborah?*, Elise Title gives her heroine amnesia, leading her to wonder if the man who claims they are married is telling the truth. Because if he's not, what on earth happened to his real wife? Lee Karr's *Stranger in the Mist* mingles past, present and future into a heady brew that will leave you guessing until the very end. And in *Swamp Secrets*, Carla Cassidy creates one of the darkest—and sexiest!—heroes I've seen in a long, long time.

And that's only the beginning! Because from now on we'll be bringing you two Shadows novels every month, novels where fear mingles with passion to create a reading experience you'll find nowhere else. And the authors who will be penning these books are some of the best anywhere. In months to come you'll find books by Jane Toombs, Helen R. Myers, Rachel Lee, Anne Stuart, Patricia Simpson, Regan Forest and Lori Herter, to name only a few. So now, step into the shadows and open yourself up to romance as you've never felt it before—on the dark side of love.

Yours,

Leslie J. Wainger
Senior Editor and Editorial Coordinator

LEE KARR

Stranger in the Mist

Published by Silhouette Books New York
America's Publisher of Contemporary Romance

SILHOUETTE BOOKS
300 East 42nd St., New York, N.Y. 10017

STRANGER IN THE MIST
Silhouette Shadows #3

Copyright © 1993 by Leona Karr

ISBN: 0-373-27003-8

First Silhouette Books printing March 1993

Printed in the U.S.A.

LEE KARR

is a native of Colorado and lives near the front range of the Rocky Mountains. She delights in being close to craggy cliffs, dramatic peaks and hidden valleys. It is no surprise that she has chosen the dramatic Rockies as the setting for *Stranger in the Mist*.

Happiest when writing and chasing new story lines, Lee is the author of more than twenty books, which include Victorian Gothics, historical romances and contemporary intrigue.

To Patricia Werner, a talented writing colleague
who has become a best friend

PROLOGUE

Lynne Delevan fell into a fitful sleep only to come awake with a jerk, her breath caught in sudden panic. The echoing emptiness of the old Victorian house had been dispelled by music and laughter floating up from the floor below. Strains of a popular tune from the mid-sixties vibrated loudly through the house. Someone was entertaining in the living room.

Apprehension and bewilderment swept through her as she grabbed her robe and slippers. This was her first night in the house and a dim light from the hall helped her navigate the unfamiliar bedroom. On some level of detached awareness, Lynne realized that the house was no longer cold but pleasantly warm. A sharp contrast to the dank chill that had greeted her upon her arrival a few hours earlier.

The music grew louder as she descended the stairs. The lower floor was bathed in a bright white light coming through the arched doorway of a large old-fashioned parlor. She crossed the wide foyer with its high, dark ceiling and walls of polished walnut wainscoting, and when she reached the open doorway of the parlor, she stopped and viewed the room with a strange detachment.

The blue-and-ivory furnishings of the room had changed. Now the drapes and rug and sofa were green, the furniture shades of brown, and a 45 rpm record player stood where a compact disc system had been. Two young women with long straight hair and wearing colorful granny dresses from the 1960s sat on a floral sofa, chatting and laughing. A gray-haired man with a muscular build leaned casually against the fireplace mantel, his face turned away so Lynne couldn't see his features. A small boy about three years old sat on a rug playing with some colorful building blocks.

The child was the only one who seemed to be aware of Lynne's presence as she stood there in the arched doorway, watching. He tipped back his head and looked directly at her. For a moment Lynne thought he was going to jump up and run toward her the way a friendly puppy would greet a newcomer, but his smile wavered and then he scrambled to the man's side and pressed close against his legs, still staring at Lynne.

The man ruffled the child's dark hair in an affectionate gesture but didn't look down at him. His attention was on the two vivacious young women, who were laughing and gesturing as they talked.

The little boy tugged on the man's hand and Lynne thought he said "Grandpa."

"Where have all the flowers gone . . . ?" The volume of the record increased to a deafening roar in Lynne's ears and the bright lucent light intensified. At the same time, an unrelenting pressure on her back thrust her forward into the room, causing her to stumble and fall in the middle of the green rug. A weird detachment engulfed her as bright colors flashed behind her closed eyelids and then swirled away as if sucked into a darkening abyss.

Slowly Lynne became aware of a blue wool rug scratching her cheek and the smell of dust in her nostrils. When she lifted her head and looked around, only the dim light from the hall shone into the darkened room. The blue-and-ivory furnishings were back. The people were gone. The record was silent and the only sound in her ears was the wind whimpering in the eaves and evergreen needles brushing against the dark windows.

CHAPTER ONE

An impression lingered in Lynne's mind when she awoke but the vague dream slipped away even as she tried to bring it into focus. What was it? She frowned and pressed her fingers against her temple. Why did she have the feeling she ought to be remembering something important? A biting iciness flowed through her, and she drew the bed covers up closer around her neck and looked around the unfamiliar bedroom with its high ceiling, old-fashioned wallpaper and heavy pieces of furniture looming darkly against the walls. A quickening wind sent moaning sounds like someone in pain down the chimney of a small fireplace and she could hear needled tree branches scraping against the outside walls. Two casement windows let in slivers of light around the edges of heavy wine-colored drapes, but the muted light did little to dispel the shadows in the room.

There was a twisting in her stomach that she couldn't analyze as she put her feet on the cold floor and stood up. An arctic chill rose from the floorboards, penetrating the soles of her feet. At that moment the house shuddered as if it were about to slip off its rock foundation in the battering wind.

Hastily she drew back one of the drapes. Jagged peaks, stark cliffs and endless dark drifts of evergreen trees met her eyes in every direction. Heavy banks of clouds still lay over the high ridges like a shroud, covering the bleak landscape. Gone were the greens of summer, and the late October scene gave little evidence that life would ever return to the dead grass and leafless scrub. There was no sign of habitation. She turned away from the window, fighting an absurd urge to walk down the stairs and straight out the door. She had never felt so displaced in all her life, and a feeling close to dread accompanied her thoughts of spending the next four weeks in the isolated house.

"You wanted quiet and solitude," she reminded herself as she took a deep breath and quickly dressed in jeans and the warm brick red sweater that her friend Dixie had said highlighted the copper tints in her russet brown hair. Dixie had been the one who had given her the idea of contacting the National House Swapping Agency and arranging to switch homes with someone for a four-week vacation. At Lynne's request the agency had sent her several names and photographs of people across the country who would be willing to live in her Chicago condo for a month while she enjoyed their home. Lynne had no intention of choosing Colorado until she saw the picture of the Victorian mansion with its dark casement windows, jagged mansard roof and arched buttress, which seemed more Gothic than Victorian. Looking at the photo, she had entertained a sense of familiarity that was utterly absurd, because she was a city gal who'd been raised in Chicago and never vacationed west of the Continental Divide. Still, she couldn't deny an undefinable urge to live in the vintage house for her month's vacation.

Arrangements for an exchange had been made with Varina Mitchell, the fiftyish widow who owned the place. As the utter silence of the house brought a cold prickling in the center of her back, Lynne wondered what kind of woman could live alone in an isolated mountain valley with the nearest town ten miles down a treacherous mountain road. Dixie would be flabbergasted to know how far I am from anything and anybody, Lynne thought as she tried to still an insidious disquiet that prickled the skin on her neck.

Just fatigue, she told herself. She'd pushed too hard on the three-day drive from Chicago and the high altitude with its oxygen-thin air was having its effect. *I just need time to adjust,* she told herself as she crossed the hall to a large bathroom complete with claw-footed tub, marble-top basin and a cupboard filled with soft lavender towels. As she dried her hands on one of them, she wondered why she thought the towels should be pink. Like a stone dropped into still water, something riffled the surface of her mind, sending ripples outward until they faded. She frowned and then shrugged.

Her footsteps echoed as she made her way down the dusky hall, glancing in shadowy rooms as she passed. The high ceiling was lost in murky darkness and a foreboding chill seemed to seep from the walls. She stopped, looked up and down the empty corridor stretching away to darkened corners. Was that the sound of a door closing?

Flickering shadows were like silent creatures listening and waiting. The sound came again. She let out her breath. The wind was moving something about on the roof, that's all.

As she descended the wide staircase, the invading emptiness of the house rushed up at her. Watery sunlight made a pale pool on the dark oak flooring of the front hall, and halfway down the steps a song flitted through her mind. "Where Have All the Flowers Gone?" She was puzzled. That old Peter, Paul and Mary classic that had been a favorite of her mother's.

Through the front door panes she could see needle-laden branches writhing in the wind and could hear the sound of their relentless scraping against the house. She started down the main hall and for some reason her steps slowed when she reached the living room's arched doorway. She looked into the room, a quivering impression lying just below the surface of her mind. Her gaze traveled around the spacious room with its dramatic marble fireplace, bright blue sofa, comfortable beige chairs, blue-and-ivory floral drapes and blue rug. The room was no different than it had been last night upon her arrival.

As she turned to go, her eyes fell on a brightly colored object lying on the rug. Her lips suddenly went dry. She was no longer cold and a hot sweat broke out on her forehead. Her heart pounded as she picked up a child's red wooden block and held it in the palm of her hand. She was startled by its warmth as her fingers closed over it. A message stirred at the back of her mind but she couldn't draw it forth. Only a child's block, she reasoned. Just a toy. Why did it bring a sense of deep disquiet? A fog seemed to be pressing down upon her, blurring her vision. With a spurt of panic, she dropped the block on a nearby table and fled the room, not knowing why she suddenly felt threatened.

When she reached the large kitchen, she chided herself for engaging in a spell of nerves. Unlike the rest of the house, the kitchen was modern in every way and quite cheery despite the dreary weather outside the large picture window. Her breathing returned to normal. What she needed was a hot cup of strong coffee. She set about making the coffee, fixing some toast and pouring a glass of orange juice. She had brought a couple of bags of groceries with her, and Varina Mitchell had said she was welcome to use any staples in the cupboards, but Lynne knew she'd have to make a trip soon to Wolverton for supplies. She wasn't looking forward to driving ten miles on the narrow twisting road scarcely wide enough for two cars. Last night, when she had driven through Wolverton's two-block business district, half of the buildings looked boarded up.

She poured a cup of coffee and walked over to the window, which overlooked a desolate hillside. A few dry leaves still clung to white-trunked aspens, and the undergrowth of dry weeds and wild grasses was dry and brittle. A gray haze hung in the air and low clouds floated down into deep craggy crevices of heavily wooded slopes.

Her eyes widened as she caught sight of some abandoned buildings clustered together along the base of the nearby mountain slopes. There must have been a ski resort in the area at some time, she thought as her gaze followed brown scars of old trails, overgrown but still visible on the mountainsides. She could make out the skeleton of a ski lift stretching upward and a few barren chairs swinging darkly against the sky. The scene was empty, silent, until a large winged bird came into view, making slow, graceful circles as it descended from a high cliff. Lynne followed its mesmerizing flight with such intent that her vision blurred. Dizzy, she shut her eyes for a split second, and when she opened them, a gray mist clouded the window glass. As it dissipated, a jolt like an electric shock went through her. The view from the window had changed.

Her heart plunged. She blinked against a sudden brightness of glistening snow and white-powder ski trails cutting through green black conifers. A flurry of activity met her eyes. The ski lift was running, the chairs were full. Skiers of all ages skimmed like multicolored birds down the runs. She was drawn into the scene and her apprehension melted away. A pleasant memory of being out on those very slopes came to her, clear and reassuring. Buttermilk Run was her favorite trail, long and not too steep. She'd always found the experience wonderfully close to flying. She delighted in the crisp air biting her cheeks and nose as she sped downhill into the wind. Her body remembered the agility and exhilaration as she banked against a curve, sending snow flying like a rooster's tail into the air.

With a catch in her throat, Lynne closed her eyes. She trembled against a memory that couldn't be. *But I don't ski!* The cry of logic came from deep within her. When she opened her eyes to the dissipating gray fog, the deserted autumn hillside had returned.

Shaken, she drew back from the window and sank down into a kitchen chair. How could she remember something that had never happened? Even the muscles of her body had for a weird moment retained the sensation of skiing. It wasn't possible—she'd never been on a ski slope! Her thoughts thrashed about in a morass of mental confusion. Why would she retain a memory that had never been a part of her experience?

A dream. A vivid daydream? Yes, that must be it. Denial was there, sharp and demanding, but she refused to acknowledge it. She drew in a shaky relieved breath. Her imagination was running overtime, that was all.

She jumped when the doorbell sounded. Until it rang a second time, she wondered if her imagination was mocking her again. Straightening her shoulders, she walked down the hall toward the front door. Her heartbeat quickened when she saw a shadow through one of the side windows. Was she hallucinating again? When she opened the door, she let out her breath. The man was real enough.

Dressed in a stylish sport jacket, an open-collar polo shirt and trim tailored slacks, he could have been waiting for his turn to tee off at a country club. Somewhere in his thirties, the man had a deeply tanned face, and midnight blue eyes surveyed her with an intensity that was immediately disconcerting.

At her startled look, he apologized in full deep tones. "I'm sorry to disturb you so early...."

Lynne stared at dark hair drifting casually on his forehead and hugging the nape of his neck. She was bewildered by a vivid sensation of having laced those dark strands through her fingers. An undefinable familiarity overtook her and she saw the same man standing in the doorway with a pair of skis balanced on his shoulders—only he was no longer a stranger. Bright sunlight splashed across banks of glittering white snow and shimmered in the crowns of nearby trees. His face was ruddy from the cold; he was laughing and his eyes were crinkled with excitement.

"How were the slopes?" she heard herself asking.

"I beg your pardon?" His bewildered look shattered the illusion. All sense of intimacy instantly dissipated. Lynne flushed in embarrassment. What on earth was the matter with her? She brushed a nervous hand across her eyes.

"This *is* the Mitchell house, isn't it?" he asked. At her nod, he smiled. "Good. I was told it was the only decent bed-and-breakfast place around. Let me introduce myself." He reached into his pocket and drew out a business card.

For a moment she didn't look at the card, as if she already knew his name. Then she took herself in hand. Of course she didn't know him. What nonsense. She read his name without any flicker of recognition. Jarrett Taylor, Investment Analyst. Santa Fe, New Mexico. That accounted for his deep western tan, she thought on one level, while on another she silently bristled. Why on earth hadn't Varina Mitchell said something about the house having been a bed-and-breakfast inn? Varina had told Lynne that she lived alone and was willing to trade for a city dwelling because it was the only way her finances could provide an extended stay in the city.

"I'd like to arrange for a few nights' lodging," he said, smiling. "My accommodations in Wolverton weren't satisfactory and I was relieved to hear about the Mitchell house."

"I'm sorry," Lynne began, searching for a way to explain. She was hugging herself against the cold as she stood in the doorway. Impulsively, she said, "Won't you come in, Mr. Taylor, and I'll try to explain the situation."

She closed the door behind him and motioned toward the living room. Then she changed her mind. Already the kitchen had become the most pleasant room in the house. "I was just having a cup of coffee...would you like to join me?"

"Sounds good."

"Kitchen's this way."

As they walked down the hall, the stranger looked about unabashedly, even reaching out to touch the carved wainscoting. "Beautiful woodwork," he said thoughtfully.

She liked the way his full voice filled the house and dispelled its gloom, and wondered what had brought him to this isolated part of Colorado. Glancing at his profile, she appreciated the strong sweep of his cheekbones and chin. A pensive look deepened the lines around his firm mouth. His forehead furrowed slightly when they entered the kitchen and his indigo eyes darkened to almost black as his gaze circled the room.

Lynne was puzzled by the intensity of his survey and the cold, unsmiling glint in his eyes. "Is something the matter?" she asked.

His expression instantly eased and his smile was apologetic. "Sorry...just can't quite match you up with this kitchen...and this house. I didn't expect someone so young to be running a bed-and-breakfast establishment."

"I'm not...and it isn't. I don't live here. I mean, not usually. It's kind of complicated. Please sit down." She took another mug from the cupboard. He accepted the coffee with a smile. "Smells wonderful."

"Sorry I don't have a cinnamon stick to make it special, the way you like it." Once the words were out, she went rigid, like someone in shock.

"How did you know I liked cinnamon coffee?" he asked quietly.

Her head started to pound and her hand trembled. She stared at the stranger. There was something undeniably familiar about the way he looked up at her, the set of his shoulders and the slight lift of his dark eyebrows. The truth was as clear as anything had ever been. *I remembered.* But it couldn't be. Jarrett Taylor didn't resemble anyone she'd ever known. Until five minutes ago, she'd never laid eyes on him. And yet she had known that he liked stirring his coffee with a cinnamon stick.

"It's all right," he assured her as she stared at him like someone caught in a frozen tableau. He reached out and touched her arm.

She drew back as the contact sent a spiral of sensation through her. Her skin prickled in remembrance.

"I'm sorry. Have I startled you in some way? I swear I'm perfectly harmless and my intentions are only the best."

Steady, girl, Lynne cautioned herself. Once again, she'd let her imagination run rampant. *So I guessed he liked cinnamon coffee.* There was a sane, logical explanation. Maybe she'd read somewhere that stirring coffee with cinnamon sticks was popular in Southwestern states—like New Mexico.

She cleared her throat, sat down at the table opposite him and gave a self-mocking laugh. "I'm not sure, Mr. Taylor, but I think you must remind me of someone." She studied his face. "Though I can't really remember who."

He responded with a half smile on his lips. "If we'd met, I would have remembered." An appreciative gaze brushed over her face and burnished hair.

Lynne couldn't deny the inexplicable intimacy ready to ignite between her and this stranger. She veered away from it. "I guess I should introduce myself. Lynne Delevan."

There was a sudden roughness in his voice as he asked, "You're not Varina Mitchell?"

Lynne shook her head. Apparently no one had told him that the the owner of the house was a widow in her fifties. "I'm from Chicago," she said.

"A member of the Mitchell family?"

"No." She felt rather foolish trying to explain how she had ended up living in this house. "Through a national house swapping agency, I agreed to exchange homes with Varina Mitchell for four weeks. I just arrived late yesterday afternoon, so I don't know anything about the house being a B and B. I'm sorry if the situation will cause you some inconvenience." She studied him frankly. "I can't help being curious—"

"About what I'm doing here?" he finished smoothly. "Business. I have a client who has been approached by some businessmen who might put the Conifer Ridge Ski Resort back in operation. I've been asked to make an evaluation."

"It looks as if it's been shut down for a long time."

"Went bankrupt over ten years ago."

Lynne was used to interacting with professional people and time slipped by as she asked questions and he gave her a succinct picture of the skiing industry. As they sipped their coffee, he talked about the problems of attracting people to a resort, the expenses involved and keeping the U.S. Forestry officials happy. Finally, he leaned back in his chair. "Enough about me. So, you're from Chicago?"

She nodded. "I have a condo on the north side. I work for the Illinois Children Social Services Division." She explained how she'd found the Mitchell house and the swap she'd made with Varina Mitchell.

"And you intend to live here alone...in this rambling house...for a month?"

She met his gaze steadily. "Yes. But I confess that I didn't realize this house was so isolated. Since the address was Wolverton, Colorado, I thought I'd be living in a small mountain community with neighbors closer than ten miles away."

"A pretty drastic change from a city like Chicago."

"I guess you could say I was experiencing the proverbial burnout on my job—too many abused children and abandoned orphans that nobody wanted. I needed to get away, and when Varina sent a photo of the house, I...I..." She searched for the right words and came up wanting. "I decided to put a little adventure in my life," she said lamely. Then she gave herself a mental shake. Why was she telling this stranger the story of her life?

"It took a lot of courage to make such a drastic change. You should have considered a state like New Mexico." He gave her an easy grin. "In my opinion, you'd have done better to take your extended vacation in a place with more sun, sand and brilliant earth colors."

"So I've been told. But the mountains have a charm of their own," she countered.

For a moment he stared out the window without answering. The furrows in his forehead deepened and his mouth tightened. His eyes were suddenly devoid of warmth. "I'd say they offer a treachery all their own."

His tone brought a soft-footed chill up her back. *You're being oversensitive,* she schooled herself.

"Would you consider renting me a room?" He leaned toward her, the smile back in his expression. She wondered if she'd been imagining the granite glare of a moment ago.

She shook her head. "I'm sorry, but I couldn't. I have to treat Varina's home the way I want her to treat mine. Besides, I signed an agreement that limits occupancy of the house to myself."

His darkly handsome face retained a pleasant expression but his eyes hinted at a guarded emotion smoldering in their depths like a hidden fire. He said smoothly, "I understand. You don't seem to be a person who would bend the rules. Ah well, I should have known finding accommodations on the site was too good to be true."

"Do you have family in Santa Fe?"

"Just my parents. Lived there all my life and never been to this part of Colorado." He sighed and looked around the kitchen. "I've always been fascinated by old houses, especially Victorian and Queen Anne architecture. We don't have anything like it in Santa Fe. Almost everything is flat and made of adobe. How old is the house, do you know?"

"I understand it was built in the 1880s by a man who struck it rich during the gold rush, but I don't know anything about its history, just that it has been in the Mitchell family for a long time."

"I bet if the walls could talk there'd be some good stories. You know, the usual . . . babies born, people dying . . . maybe even a murder or two."

She tried to keep her tone light. "Are you warning me against ghosts?" Unconsciously her tongue flicked some moisture on her dry lips.

He leaned across the table. "Do you know that your eyes flicker from blue to gray in a most fascinating way sometimes?"

She chided herself for the way her cheeks instantly flamed with warmth. Since when did a compliment about the color of her eyes bring a foolish rippling to her skin? He was probably hoping flattery would make her change her mind about the room. "Would you like another cup of coffee?" she asked politely.

He sighed. "No, I'd better be going. I have a lot of work to do. Checking out all the legal aspects and such. Does Mrs. Mitchell live here by herself all the time?"

"I don't know."

"Must get pretty cold in the winter."

"The house doesn't seem to warm up even now," Lynne admitted.

"An old house like this is hard to heat. Would you like me to take a look at the furnace? I don't suppose you've been down the cellar to check it out."

"I wouldn't know what to check," Lynne admitted.

"I'd be glad to take a look... if you'd like?"

She hesitated. Maybe there was something wrong with the heating system. "Well, if it wouldn't be too much trouble..."

"Not at all."

"Is that the basement door?" He walked across the room and opened a solid wooden door. "Yes, this is it."

Lynne followed him halfway down some steep, narrow steps and then stopped as the fusty-smelling, dark cavern swallowed him up. She turned around and came back to the kitchen. She was beginning to get uneasy when he finally appeared with a smudge of dirt on his face.

"Everything looks fine," he said. "Clean filter. A good strong unit that should provide plenty of hot air to all the rooms."

"I'm afraid you're taking away some of the dirt with you." She gently wiped away the smudge on his face with a towel. As her fingers touched his cheek, their eyes met and held. Her breathing suddenly became shallow. Her senses reeled from his nearness. She fought a bewildering force like an undertow drawing them together. An overwhelming urge to surrender herself to him brought an embarrassing warmth to her face. She stepped back hastily and stammered, "There...it's okay now."

He searched her eyes. "I guess I'd better go."

She nodded and avoided meeting his gaze.

"Do you believe in things happening over which we have no control?" he asked in a soft persuasive tone.

There was no reason to give the question dark significance. She'd heard a line like that many times before and it was silly to respond with a surge of breathless tension. She needed to say something light and dismissing, but she didn't want him to leave, didn't want to be alone. She found herself saying, "I was planning on getting acquainted with the house this morning. Would you like a tour?"

He smiled as if he'd known all along she wasn't ready for him to leave. "Where shall we begin?"

There was an expectant excitement as they covered the main floor, finding a pleasant library and dining room in addition to the front parlor. A pair of double doors at the end of one hall was locked.

"Maybe a game room or den," he speculated. "I wonder why Mrs. Mitchell locked it up." He sounded disappointed.

Lynne shrugged and went on down the hall. Thick trees crowded the windows of an empty conservatory, shut off sunlight and obliterated any view of the surrounding hillside. There was no sign that any plants had been grown in it for years. A musty unpleasant smell made Lynne grateful to shut the room up again.

At the end of a back hall off the kitchen they found servants' quarters. Lynne was surprised to find one of the rooms nicely furnished as a small bedroom with a tiny bath across the hall. A short distance beyond, a staircase twisted upward.

"Servants' stairs," said Jarrett.

The narrow passage was dark and dusty and Lynne hesitated, but he put a firm hand on her back and urged her forward. The door at the top was closed and the passage grew darker as they mounted the steep stairs. The walls seemed to crowd in closer with each step. A rush of panic made her stumble as she lunged forward, scrambling upward. It was an eternity before she finally reached the top step and frantically turned the doorknob. At first the door wouldn't open, but she gave it a vicious shove and burst into the upper hall, gasping for air.

"Are you all right?" He reached out to steady her, but she drew back.

His eyes narrowed in concern. "I'm sorry...I didn't realize. You should have told me you were claustrophobic."

"I'm not. It's just that...," she faltered. How could she explain the sudden rush of panic she'd experienced? Once more the house seemed to be darkly alive, hiding some evil truth that was about to reach out and trap her. She turned away abruptly, embarrassed by her melodramatic behavior. "Shall we get on with the tour?"

"Horrendous wallpaper," he said as he poked his head in the door of her bedroom and viewed the fuchsia cabbage roses.

"I know, but I think it's the room Varina wanted me to use. I found extra covers folded on the bed."

At the end of the hall, they found another locked door, which Lynne speculated must be Varina's room.

"Shall we take a look in the attic?" he asked, purposefully walking back down the hall to a second closed door beyond the main staircase, that Lynne had taken to be a broom closet.

For a moment she couldn't find her voice. She stood stunned as he opened the door without hesitation, revealing a set of narrow stairs leading upward.

She stared at him in disbelief, a sudden roar like a devil's wind in her ears. "How did you know that door led to the attic?"

CHAPTER TWO

Jarrett's eyes flashed with a sharpness that was in contrast to his reasonable tone as he replied, "I guess I just assumed that since the back stairs opened at this end of the hall, the attic stairs must be close by."

Lynne realized then that at no time during their tour of the house had he indicated a moment's hesitancy as they climbed stairs, walked the halls or looked out windows. He had been much more at ease in the unfamiliar surroundings than she.

"Do you want to skip the attic?" he asked in that same matter-of-fact tone.

When she didn't answer, he closed the door and walked back to her. He searched her face as if speculating why the companionable mood between them had dissipated so suddenly.

She lowered her eyes, ill at ease under his scrutiny. What on earth was the matter with her? Why had she reacted as if there were some sinister interpretation to his opening the correct door to the attic? His company had dispelled the depression she had felt earlier, and she was more comfortable in the house than at any time since her arrival.

"I have a feeling I've overstayed my welcome," he said quietly.

"No, not at all," she answered quickly, looking up at him. "I've enjoyed having company... and... and I think I'll be able to settle in more comfortably now that I've toured the house." She gave him a weak smile. "But I'll pass on the attic. I'm not up to cobwebs and spiders," she admitted frankly.

As they walked down the main staircase, he looked over the banister and then up at the vaulted ceiling. "Thank you for indulging my curiosity. There's something about the house that's very... engaging."

She was certain he was about to use another adjective. Brooding, perhaps? Eerie? Disquieting? She touched a hand to her forehead, trying to understand why her thoughts and memories were whirling about on some kind of mental Ferris wheel.

"You look tired," he said, watching her expression.

"I—I didn't sleep well last night." She walked with him to the door. "I still have to unload my car."

"Let me give you a hand."

A flicker of warning was there in the shadows of her mind, but she ignored it. A strange sense of relief sluiced through her. "Thanks. I'd appreciate it."

His intense blue eyes bore into hers. "My pleasure."

They made nearly a dozen trips back and forth, bringing in all the personal possessions she thought she couldn't live a month without.

"You seem to be handy around the house," Lynne observed as he deftly found room in a glass-fronted bookcase for the dozen or so books she had brought along. "Someone must have trained you well."

"My mother has always worked—both she and my father are teachers—so I learned quite early to do my share." He shut the glass door of the bookcase and then grinned at her as if he knew exactly what she was really asking. "I've never been married. How about you? Any husbands back in Chicago, current or past?"

"Married to my job, I'm afraid."

"Then we're a matched pair, I'd say."

She tried to quell the unspoken communication that flowed effortlessly between them. Her training in psychology had made her always sensitive to body language and outward manifestations of hidden emotions, but she knew that there was something deeper between them than a superficial acquaintance. A few hours ago she had not known of his existence and now his presence in the house seemed irrevocably meshed with her own. She knew that once he walked out of the house, the insidious chill would be back.

"I'll build a fire so you can read in comfort," he said, stooping in front of the library fireplace and coaxing kindling and paper into a warm blaze. "We use fireplaces a lot in New Mexico. Takes the chill off the house. And watching flames dancing across a log soothes the mind." He stared at the fire and added thoughtfully, "Expands an awareness of life's mysteries."

Dark hair drifting forward around his face softened the bold lines of his profile. A man who could be as ruthless as he could be gentle, thought Lynne. A jutting line to his chin warned that his pleasant smile and easy manner could be deceptive. There was a tensile strength in the hard sinews of his neck and shoulders and she knew better than to take him at face value as her gaze followed the strong curve of his back and the smooth planes of his waist and thighs. She remembered the impression that had overtaken her when she opened the door, and the incident with the cinnamon stick...as if he were a part of some subconscious memory.

He stood up, watched the crackling flames for a few moments in silence, then turned to look at her. The intensity of his eyes made her stiffen against a physical attraction that had flared the moment she saw him. Her vulnerability in the strange surroundings sounded a warning that her judgment could be impaired. Inviting a perfect stranger to live in the house with her was utterly irresponsible...and dangerous. Even as she lectured herself, she admitted defeat. She must have been changing her mind all the time they brought her belongings in the house.

"Perhaps you could have the back room...for a few nights. Of course, I'll have to telephone Varina Mitchell," she added quickly, "and explain the situation."

His smile was slow, bathing her face with warmth that flowed through her veins like brandy. "I won't be any trouble."

Some mocking voice taunted her that he had promised nothing but trouble from the moment he had walked through the door.

When Lynne telephoned her condo in Chicago and reached Varina Mitchell, the woman was less than pleased. Furious was more like it. "How dare you turn my home into a boardinghouse? I can't believe you would think it would be agreeable to me. All the years I've been a widow, I've never even considered such a thing."

"But Mr. Taylor said that someone in Wolverton told him that the Mitchell house was a bed-and-breakfast place."

"That was years ago, in the sixties, before my husband died. Who is this man you've taken into my house?"

"His name is Jarrett Taylor. He's an investment analyst from Santa Fe, New Mexico, looking over the ski resort for a client."

There was a moment of weighted silence.

"Really? Someone's interested in the Conifer Ridge Ski Resort? Did he say who the investor was?"

"No."

Another poignant pause. "Well now, that's very interesting. I'd given up hope of ever getting back a penny on that venture. Maybe I better call my lawyer. Have him do a little checking on Mr. Taylor. I'd really like to know who's behind this sudden interest in the resort." Varina's tone had changed completely. Now it was brisk and businesslike, all anger gone. "All right, let him stay. But you're to keep me posted," she ordered, as if there had never been any question about letting the stranger rent a room in her house. "How long is he staying?"

"Just a few days, I think. I realize that I've overstepped our agreement—"

"Under the circumstances, I guess we can overlook your impetuous behavior." The woman's tone was conciliatory. "I must admit that I'm enjoying being back in civilization. Before I lost money in that damn resort, I used to make yearly treks to New York, Chicago and Los Angeles. I could afford the best hotels then." She sighed. "But I won't be spending much time in your condo, comfortable as it is. I plan to be on the go every minute that I can. Well, dearie, take care of things... and watch yourself with Mr. Taylor." Her chuckle had a smirk in it.

Jarrett didn't seem surprised that Varina had approved of his staying in the house. He asked if he could work in the library and make his telephone calls from there.

"Of course." She left him spreading out papers and maps on the library table, and heard him talking on the phone as she busied herself in the kitchen. At lunchtime, she told him there were sandwich makings on the table. He said "Thanks" and went on working.

She ate alone and then went upstairs to her room. She'd done the right thing, hadn't she? After all, asking him to stay had been her decision. There wasn't any reason for her to feel that she'd been manipulated.

She curled up on her bed under a weight of covers and tried to get warm. The temperature in the house seemed to rise and fall with illogical variation... either pleasantly warm or filled with a penetrating chill. She closed her heavy eyelids. Strangely content, she fell asleep.

* * *

When she awoke, dusky shadows filled the room. Was it night or early morning? For a moment she was disoriented. Huge cabbage roses on the wallpaper had lost their shape. The bed's heavy, ornate headboard loomed above her head. Something moved in the reflection of the large mirror as she sat up. It took her a moment to realize that the shadowy face staring back at her was her own.

The sound of someone moving around downstairs reached her ears. *Jarrett.* She turned on the bedside lamp and saw that her clock read six-fifteen. She'd been asleep for nearly four hours.

Hurriedly brushing her hair and touching some color to her lips, she went downstairs, almost afraid she would discover that Jarrett's presence in the house was another imaginary illusion. When she found him in the kitchen, staring at a nearly empty refrigerator, she gave a breathless laugh of relief.

She fixed them a rather plain meal of broiled pork chops and brown rice, which she had planned for herself. "I'll have to make a grocery list and do some marketing."

"You won't find much of a market in Wolverton," he told her. "Tell you what. I have to drive to White Springs, the county seat, tomorrow. I have some records to look up. Why don't you give me a list and let me pick up the groceries? I might even throw a few things into the cart and treat you to one of my culinary specialties tomorrow evening."

"Like veal *dijonnaise?*" Sparks like those from a frayed electrical cord went through her. *How did I know that?*

He slowly laid down his fork. "You astound me. How did you know that veal *dijonnaise* is my specialty?" He raised a dark eyebrow. "Are you a mind reader, pretty lady? If you are, I'll have to manage some kind of mental censorship when I'm with you or you'll be slapping my face more often than you know."

Her mouth was dry. "I seem to have a memory of you cooking that meal...right here...in this very kitchen." Her head was strangely light with unfocused images in her mind.

"A vivid imagination, that's what it is," he said lightly, but there was a puzzled edge to the reassurance. "I have a writer friend who tells me that happens to him all the time."

"Really?"

"Really. Now stop looking at me with those watery sea blue eyes—" his tone softened "—or you won't have to guess what I'm thinking."

Even as she stared at him, her ears echoed with remembered whispered endearments. In some unfathomable way, she had felt the caressing touch of his hands and had known the warmth of his kisses in the soft cleft of her neck. She knew the possessive passion of his lovemaking. The memory was sharp, undeniable—and it had never happened!

"It's all right. Don't look so frightened," he ordered in a firm voice. "I'm sorry. My mistake. Let's talk about something else." Very deliberately he cut into his chop and began eating as if he had nothing more important on his mind than enjoying the meal.

She felt him watching her. A coolness on her forehead told her that beads of sweat had formed there. She covered her eyes for a moment with her hand, took a deep breath to steady her breathing. He was a stranger...someone she had barely known for a day. How could she have memories of him that were intimate and passionate? Was she guilty of fantasizing because she found him attractive? That must be it. She felt utterly foolish. Her smile was rather sheepish, but the inner turmoil was gone. She was in control again. "Tell me, what does a financial analyst do?"

"Advise. And we try to keep our eyes on the big financial picture." He deepened his voice in a comical way and asked with mock solemnity, "What do you think about the world's monetary system, Miss Delevan? Do you think we should be exchanging our dollars for yens?"

She gave a shaky laugh. "Only if Japan buys up McDonald's and Burger King."

The flippant remark led into a discussion of world monetary problems and away from personal revelations. They were having coffee in the library when the conversation turned more personal once again.

The impression that she had known Jarrett before faded completely. He had gone to the University of Arizona, played football, graduated with a business degree and worked in an investment office in Phoenix before returning to Santa Fe to start his own business.

In response to his questions, she admitted that she was a city girl through and through, had taken her degrees at the University of Chicago, renowned for its social work program. She'd worked for Cook County most of her professional life.

"Funny that our paths should cross at all," he said, thoughtfully.

She remembered the pull that the photo of this house had had for her. How much was coincidence—and how much was fate? She gave herself a mental shake. Metaphysical questions had never been her strong point. Her life had been anything but obtuse or fanciful—until now. "I think I'll clean up and then call it a day," she said, standing.

"I'll help. Thanks for the dinner...and the company."

When they were finished, he walked with her to the foot of the stairs.

She hesitated before mounting the first step. He touched her arm lightly with his fingertips. She turned and looked up at him. A mesmerizing intensity radiated from his eyes, deep as cobalt and feathered by a fringe of dark lashes. His fingers tightened gently on her arm and she responded to the pressure by leaning toward him. His lips parted slightly in the hint of a smile.

"Good night," he said softly.

Caught in a spill gate of emotions, she echoed, "'Night."

His eyelids lowered as he bent his head, bringing his lips inches from her own. His kiss was waiting, taunt-

ing her with the warmth of his breath and half-closed
midnight eyes. She leaned into his strength and her lips
quivered as she accepted his mouth, gently measured
yet filled with all the force of an exploding rocket.
When he lifted his lips, she wavered unsteadily for a
moment.

"Good night," he said again, this time dropping his
arms and stepping back in a gentlemanly fashion. The
promise in his eyes warned her that he was not im-
mune to temptation.

She turned and took the stairs in a firm, deliberate
pace, a contrast to an inner sensation that she was
floating up the staircase.

She heard him checking on doors and turning out
lights before he retired to his room. Shaking from the
intensity of his kiss, she settled herself in bed, closed
her eyes and tried not to think about the explosive attraction she felt for this stranger who had entered her
life only a few hours earlier. What was the matter with
her that her emotions were reeling like a Fourth of July
pinwheel? She touched her lips, still warm and quivering. *I shouldn't let him stay.* On some level of
awareness, she sensed that the decision wasn't really
hers. Something beyond rational understanding had
brought him to this house.

She turned on the light and tried reading but her
thoughts kept slipping back to the handsome Jarrett
Taylor sleeping on the floor below. *What made her
think she'd known him before?* How could she explain
those remembered flashes of intimacy?

Sighing, she turned out the light. The house was no longer cold and a radiating warmth seemed to seep from the walls. Peculiar, she thought as she drifted off to sleep.

She awoke with the aroma of coffee teasing her nostrils. Raising her arms above her head, she stretched leisurely, a smile curving her lips as she remembered the pleasant evening she'd had getting acquainted with her lodger. She felt refreshed and full of energy as she threw back the covers, chagrined to find it was already eight-thirty.

She showered quickly, noting that the house was warmer than it had ever been, then dressed in cream-colored slacks and a yellow pullover with a V-neck. She touched her lips with pink lipstick, secured her russet hair in a long barrette at the nape of her neck and nodded at her reflection in a lovely floor-standing oval mirror. It framed her lithe figure and she gave a satisfied pat to her flat tummy. Thank heavens for the hours she'd spent every week at her exercise club. She bounded down the steps with the energy of a young filly.

"I'm sorry," she apologized as she entered the kitchen and found bacon cooked, coffee made and bread in the toaster waiting to be browned. "I think you have the wrong idea about a bed-and-breakfast. The guests aren't supposed to make the breakfast."

"Not even when the lady of the house is a disgraceful sleepyhead?" he said with a teasing glint in his blue eyes, frankly appraising the sweep of red brown hair and the smooth curve of her cheeks and slender neck. "You're looking much better this morning. Not so wan and pale . . . and jumpy."

"Thanks—I think." She surveyed his pin-striped shirt, tie, gray trousers and the tweed jacket that he had placed on the back of his chair. Her heart instantly tightened. "You're about ready to leave?"

"Yep." He finished his coffee and put on his jacket. "Not looking forward to spending the day in a dusty courthouse. What are you going to do?"

"Just rest."

"Good idea." He hesitated. "Will you be all right?"

She laughed. "Good heavens. I've survived the daily perils of Chicago all by myself. I can certainly manage to exist in seclusion."

He didn't return her smile. "A city girl might get the heebie-jeebies being all alone in this place. Don't do anything that might prove dangerous." His voice held a warning.

Lynne bristled at his dictatorial tone. "I hardly think I'll run into any problems reading and sleeping. I came here for *solitude*." She landed a little harder on the word than she had intended and she saw his mouth tighten. She was instantly contrite. "But thanks for your concern."

He touched her cheek lightly. "Take care."

"I will."

The kiss he placed on her cheek was light and casual, not like last night's flaming contact. Then he turned and left quickly as if he were tempted to linger.

The house seemed to lose its warmth after he was gone. Nonsense, she told herself. She'd always been good company for herself—too much so, according to her friend Dixie. Oh, there had been male company when she wanted it. Even a couple of intense relationships, but in the end, she'd never found anyone for that "happy-ever-after" state that everyone talked about.

Briskly, she set out doing kitchen chores, then went upstairs and straightened her room. After lunch she settled herself in the library, which had already become the room she preferred. Jarrett had left business papers scattered on the oak desk and she was grateful for the mess because the clutter was a tangible sign that he would return. She emptied ashes from the fireplace and built another fire.

For the second day the weather was gray and dismal, so she drew the library drapes, shutting out an icy rain that peppered the windowpanes. She wandered about the library, looking at dusty books; none was published recently and all seemed pedantic. An old-fashioned windup clock ticked away the seconds with excruciating slowness.

Lynne stared at the fire, sent impatient glances at the clock and turned pages of her book without reading any of it. When five o'clock came, she began listening for Jarrett's return. Six o'clock ticked by and the muscles in her neck began to tighten. Where was he? He'd said would be back in time to fix dinner.

Restless, she made trips to the front door, peering out through the windows, searching for some flash of headlights in the thickening rain and darkness. The utter silence of the approaching night was unnerving. She missed the sounds of traffic, the roar of jets, the loud stereo blaring from her next-door neighbor's window. City noises that had been irritating to her would have been comforting in this alien setting.

Wandering into the living room, she tried tuning in a small radio but all she got was static. She turned it off with an exasperated twist. No TV, of course. Then she began looking through record albums stacked in a modern console and found several offerings from Barbra Streisand, Neil Diamond and Kenny Rogers. Thank heavens Varina had similar tastes in music, she thought as she chose "September Morn," and Neil Diamond's deep voice reassuringly filled the room.

Sitting down on the sofa, she spied the red block that lay on the end table. She hadn't come upon any other toys or children's belongings as she toured the house with Jarrett. Funny, she thought. Why would one lone block be left on the living room rug? She idly picked it up.

Its red color deepened with a radiating warmth as it nestled in the palm of her hand. A mesmerizing brightness caused her to blink and she suddenly felt light-headed. Startled, she let the block tumble from her hand.

Her head began to pound. Her lips went dry and cold, clammy perspiration broke out on the palms of her hands. She narrowed her eyes against a fog that pressed against her. She closed her eyes as a bright bluish light blinded her. When she opened them, she was no longer alone.

A little boy stood in the middle of a green rug playing with a brown teddy bear. His tiny mouth was spread in a wide grin as he looked at her, his face round with baby fat and his wide blue eyes fringed with long dark lashes.

A dreamlike lassitude enveloped Lynne. The cushions of the floral sofa were soft, and a green crocheted pillow supported her back in a comfortable fashion. She sat there, content to watch the child throw his stuffed animal up in the air with childish glee, then twirl around until he collapsed in a fit of giggles on the floor.

She felt herself laughing with him but could hear no sound coming from her lips or the little boy's. She clapped her soundless hands as he did a couple of wobbly somersaults.

Grinning, he picked up his teddy bear and held it out to her. Then his gaze shifted to some point over her head. With wide-eyed fright, he began to back away. She saw his mouth round in a silent cry. The terror in his eyes was like that of a trapped animal.

A blast of glacial air hit the back of Lynne's neck and her hair whipped across her face. Fog poured over her like the crest of a vaporous wave, sucking her under and then finally shooting her back to the surface.

Hot sweat ran down her face and throat. She was trembling as she looked around the room with its beige rug and blue furniture. Was she awake? Was she caught in the horrible state of thinking she was awake when she was still dreaming? She pressed her fingers against her temples. Her head was aching and she couldn't remember. An elusive memory like a shadow passed across her mind. Frantically she tried to grasp it but the impression slipped past her—leaving only a whisper of evil lying cold upon her flesh.

Above the strains of the Neil Diamond record, she heard the high-pitched, insistent ringing of the library telephone.

CHAPTER THREE

She was still trembling when she reached the library and croaked a shaky "Hello" into the phone.

"What's wrong, Lynne?" Jarrett demanded. "You sound sick."

Sick? A hot flush coated her hands and face, yet she was shivering as if she were chilled to the core. Adrenaline fired every nerve in her body. Her thoughts floundered in some bewildering emotional morass. *What's wrong with me?* A frightening impression lingered in her mind but already its intensity was fading, receding like a wave curling back on itself and disappearing. She couldn't bring the image forth.

"For God's sake, Lynne, talk to me."

"I'm sorry, I..."

"Is somebody there with you?"

She worried her lower lip. "No, I'm alone."

"Are all the doors locked?"

She gripped the telephone receiver tighter and forced herself to respond in a reasonable tone. "Yes, the doors are locked." *How can locked doors keep out a malevolent force that's already inside?*

"Then what's the matter? Something's wrong, I know it."

She moistened her dry lips.

"What's the matter?" he asked again.

Taking a deep breath, she tried to explain as her mind scurried to make sense of what had happened. "I was sitting on the sofa...in the living room...listening to a Neil Diamond record...and—" She faltered.

"Yes?"

The lines of worry in her forehead eased, and she gave a weak laugh. The answer was so simple she was almost too embarrassed to admit it. A bad dream! Nightmares often caused hot sweats, a dry mouth and a bewildering sense of displacement. That must be it. Her voice was stronger as relief eased her taut nerves. "I must have fallen asleep on the sofa," she told him. "And the telephone woke me...right in the middle of a nightmare."

"Well, it must have been a doozy. You sound pretty shaken up."

"Yes," she admitted. "I'm still shaking. My heart is thumping, my hands are sweaty. Why am I reacting so strongly to something I can't remember? My memory's like a blank screen."

"That's the way with dreams," he said in a matter-of-fact tone. "Probably just as well."

"But I feel that it's important for me to remember," she protested.

"Most nightmares are better forgotten."

"I'd rather remember," she argued.

"Well, maybe you will...and maybe you won't. The subconscious has a way of protecting itself." His voice softened. "Anyway, you really had me going for a minute. I couldn't imagine...well, I'm glad it was just a dream. From what you've said, I'd guess that some anxiety about the house is coming to the fore when you're asleep. Such a drastic change of life-style is bound to create some apprehension. You'll just need a little while to settle in and get comfortable, Lynne, that's all. Nothing to get uptight about.''

His tone was rather patronizing. No need to treat her like some child afraid of the dark, assuring her there were no boogeymen. Choking back a quick retort, she glanced up at the clock. ''Where are you? It's nearly six-thirty.''

''I know. I tried to finish up so I wouldn't have to stay over in White Springs, but my meeting with the county commissioners ran late. I'm going to get a motel for the night. Still plenty of data that has to be nailed down. Hopefully I can finish up tomorrow.''

''I see.'' *He's not coming.* Disappointment mingled with unreasonable anger. She chided herself for depending upon a glib, charming man for support when she'd always prided herself on enjoying solitude.

''I did my best to hurry things along,'' he explained, as if sensing her disappointment.

''That's all right. After all, you're here on business. I'm sure you're anxious to finish up and get back to New Mexico.''

''Not as anxious as you might think.''

Even over the phone, his voice had a soft, stroking timbre that did crazy things to her. All day she had foolishly organized her thoughts around the meal he was going to cook and the evening they would spend together. Not only was such anticipation stupid—but it was dangerous. She'd better get herself in hand, and quick.

"What's the weather like?" he asked, as if trying to keep her on the line.

"Icy rain."

"Here, too. Maybe it will turn to snow before morning."

Her chest tightened. She'd expected some winter storms, but not so soon. What if the narrow mountain road between the house and Wolverton was closed? She wasn't prepared to be isolated. She wasn't prepared for a lot of things, she thought wryly.

"Lynne, I really am sorry."

"You don't have to apologize to me." Her tone was quite brisk. She knew she was being unreasonable but anger was a good antidote for fear. She needed to lash out at something or someone. Jarrett Taylor seemed ready-made. "It seems to me you'd find it more convenient to stay in White Springs . . . all the time."

"I don't think so," he answered evenly.

"Why not?"

He hesitated. "Are you having second thoughts?" he asked evasively.

"Actually, it doesn't matter to me one way or another."

"I'm sorry to hear that." His intimate tone was in contrast to her briskness. "I was looking forward to more of your company."

He's too darn smooth, she thought. "Why are you so insistent on staying here? It seems to me you'd save yourself a lot of driving if you stayed in White Springs.''

There was a pause as if he were weighing his words. ''I think it would be better for me to be close to the site. I'd do a better job of interpreting the old maps. I hope you haven't really changed your mind about the room.''

''I don't go back on my commitments.''

''I'm glad. From your tone I wouldn't be surprised to find my stuff thrown out in the road when I come back.'' He gave a soft chuckle. ''I should have known that a temper went with that fiery brown hair.''

''I don't have a temper.''

''Good. For a minute there I had the feeling you were ready to throw rotten eggs at me.''

''You're safe.'' Her tone softened. ''I'm out of eggs.''

He laughed. ''Sounds as if you might have missed my company today.''

An instinctive warning that he knew how vulnerable she was at the moment made her reply coolly, ''Sorry to disappoint you. I spent a very pleasant day in the house.''

''I really planned to get back with some groceries. I promise I'll bring food and wine for tomorrow night.''

''I'll understand if it doesn't work out.''

''Lynne, are you all right?'' His tone was soft enough to be a caress.

The memory of his good-night kiss flared up in her. She was glad he couldn't see the warmth that suffused her face. She'd never had her emotions put into such a

tailspin by a man before. She was irritated with herself—and him. "I'm fine, thank you. I'll see you when
you get back." She hung up with a punctuating click.

She had herself under control now. The fact that she
had been hurt and disappointed when she knew Jarrett wasn't coming was due to the displacement she felt
in the house. She certainly wasn't foolish enough to
allow herself to become romantically entangled with a
man she'd met twenty-four hours ago.

Her steps were brisk and firm as she moved about
the kitchen, preparing a meal of baked chicken and
vegetables. She ate at the kitchen table, determined not
to give in to the desolate sound of the rain against the
window and the irritating scraping of branches against
the house.

The empty chair across from her mocked the lie that
she was perfectly content with her solitary meal. Was
it only this morning that he had sat there, his dark eyes
responding to her in a way that denied any strangeness
between them? Why did she have the impression that
he was no stranger? She still didn't understand why she
had fantasized him standing at the front door with skis
on his shoulder. It must have been caused by the daydream she'd had a few minutes earlier when looking
out the window. Her fantasy of skiing had been really
absurd. Buttermilk Run...wasn't that the name her
mind had created?

Maybe the high altitude and thin air were causing the
nightmares and daydreams. Lynne had heard of high
altitude sickness, but she didn't know it brought about
such fantasies of the mind. She almost feared that if

she looked across the table at the vacant chair she would see Jarrett sitting there, the flicker of a smile on his lips and in his wonderfully midnight blue eyes. The empty kitchen echoed with the sound of his voice and she smiled to herself, remembering how nice last night's companionship had been.

After rinsing her plate and placing it in a rack to dry, she left the kitchen and returned to the library. There were only three logs left in the wood carrier. She'd have to check and see if there was any wood stacked outside. But not tonight. The wind whined plaintively at the windows and the house shuddered with creaks and groans. She put another log on the fire, sat down with a book in her hand and then tossed it aside.

Impulsively, she reached for the phone and called her friend and co-worker.

"Greetings from Colorado," Lynne said in a falsely bright tone when she had Dixie on the line.

"Well, hello, gypsy," said Dixie in her slow Southern way. "Was just thinking about you...wondering if you got there safe and sound. Tell me everything. Did you make a good trade?"

"It's not quite what I expected," Lynne hedged. "High ceilings, dark rooms, a dank cold feeling that goes bone-deep. And it's ten miles from the nearest town."

"You sound as nervous as frog legs frying," Dixie said with her usual frankness. "I thought swapping houses would put some excitement in your life. Blast it all, anyone could see you needed a well-deserved break from work."

"Dixie, did you think that...that I was...that my nerves were...that I was heading for a nervous breakdown?"

"A nervous breakdown? Like you were about to flip your lid or something?" She laughed. "What kind of question is that? You needed a rest, period. And I wanted to see you get something in your life besides work. A pretty gal like you should be thinking about something besides other people's kids, endless case studies and court orders night and day." She sighed. "I guess my suggestion that you switch houses with someone backfired."

Lynne started to tell her about Jarrett and then changed her mind. Even though Dixie wanted her to meet eligible men, Lynne knew her friend would explode if she told her she had been persuaded to allow a perfect stranger to live under the same roof. Nobody with any sense opened her doors to someone she didn't know. *But I know him,* Lynne thought with bizarre certainty.

"Is something going on that you're not telling me? You always were a terrible liar. There's something in your voice...."

"Must be a bad connection," said Lynne flippantly. "How are things at work going?"

"Same squirrel cage as usual." Dixie filled her in on office gossip and the resolution of some cases that had been pending. As they talked, Lynne felt as if she'd been away from the job for weeks instead of days. Dixie assured her that everything was under control.

"Don't worry about anything here. Put the job out of your mind. Getting out from under all the pressures was the whole idea."

"Yes, that was the idea."

Her sarcastic edge made Dixie ask, "You're going to be all right, aren't you? I mean, the house is livable, isn't it? If it isn't, you can break the contract."

"There's nothing wrong with the house."

"Well, it sounds like you were misled about the house and the town. What's a big house like that doing in the middle of nowhere? Good heavens, what kind of a mess have you gotten yourself into, girl? You'd better hightail it back here before that woman gets settled in your condo. Tell her it was all a mistake... that she misrepresented the situation."

"Too late. I can't go back on our signed agreement. Besides, I talked to Varina yesterday and she's satisfied with the exchange. There's nothing I can do but accept the situation."

"Well, the place sounds like a set in a bad movie. Could drive anybody nuts, if you ask me."

Lynne swallowed back the temptation to tell Dixie everything—the fantasies, the nightmares that she couldn't remember and the malevolent chill of the house. *And what good would that do?* Lynne knew she'd just worry her friend. How could she explain to Dixie what was going on when she didn't have a clue herself?

"It's going to be... interesting," said Lynne lamely.

Dixie snorted. "I hate that word. What in blazes does 'interesting' mean?"

"I guess we'll just have to wait and see," Lynne parried.

"Well, you keep me up-to-date, hear?"

Lynne promised that she would. After she hung up, she was sorry she hadn't completely leveled with Dixie about Jarrett. Ah well, maybe she'd write a letter—later.

She read until the fire died down. Then she went upstairs to her cold bedroom. Determined to maintain her nightly rituals, she slipped on her flannel gown and stood in front of the oval mirror while she vigorously brushed her hair until the bronze strands lay shining on her shoulders. Looking at the reflection of her oval face and blue-gray eyes, she allowed a smile to curve her lips. Vanity had never been one of her faults but she had never lied to herself. She had no quarrel with the unique color of her eyes, or the slender shape of her nose, the curve of her cheekbones and a slight cleft in her chin. *Your breasts were made for a lover's touch.*

She stiffened. The whispered words were a clue to a memory that flitted just beyond her reach.

As she stared wide-eyed into the mirror, it clouded with a misty vapor. A diffusion of light narrowed her vision, and like someone disappearing into a fog, her reflected figure blurred and faded. Dizziness caused her to put a hand on the tall frame for support until the silvered glass cleared and her vision returned.

She stared again at her reflection in the mirror. Her shoulder-length hair still shone like burnished bronze but no longer was she wearing a high-necked flannel gown. Her body was draped in a seductive creamy satin nightgown. Slowly, she raised her gaze, and met Jarrett's eyes in the mirror.

"Beautiful," he whispered, and his warm breath lightly brushed her skin. With tantalizing fingertips, he slipped the narrow straps off her shoulders and let his lips softly nuzzle the nape of her neck and shoulders.

She leaned back against him, welcoming an arousal that quickened her breathing. His tongue lightly tasted the sweetness of her skin and her color rose as a heady warmth sped through her. She savored the desire unfolding within her.

He guided the luminous satin down over her smooth stomach, thighs and legs until the fabric fell with a soft whisper around her bare feet. In the mirror, his indigo eyes smiled at her. Very deliberately his warm gaze caressed her nakedness. Every inch of her skin vibrated with sensual anticipation as his hands slipped to her waist and he drew her back against his body as if drawing her into himself.

She knew what it was like to lie in bed with him, to be filled with his warmth, to hear the hard pounding of his heart and feel his quickened breath upon her face. The heat and strength of his body were vibrant and commanding. Slowly, she turned around, ready for his kiss, eager to appease the unfolding hunger that he had always satisfied. She held out her arms—to air.

The floor dipped as if it had just dropped out from under her. She couldn't get her breath. Sparks of color whirled in front of her like riotous dots in a sea of darkness. Her hands clutched the folds of the flannel gown. She shivered as the fiery warmth of a lover's touch drained away from her. Even as she tried to hold the moment in the present, some out-of-rhyme continuum of time swept it away from her.

Lynne threw herself on the bed and wept. "I was *not* hallucinating. I was *not* dreaming."

I was remembering!

CHAPTER FOUR

When Lynne awoke the next morning, the dream still lingered in her mind. No, *not* a dream, she silently protested. She'd been wide-awake when she had looked into the mirror and met Jarrett's eyes. And she rejected the idea that she had been fantasizing. The images had too much depth and intense emotion not to have a reality beyond her own mind. Every sensation, every emotion, every touch brought an awareness of something remembered. The rapturous desire was not new to her, nor were the familiar shooting spasms of delight as he trailed kisses on her tingling skin. Her body had recognized the warmth of his virile frame as she leaned back against him. They were all remembered sensations. *Remembered from a time past*. But it couldn't be. How could she have such a vivid memory of a passionate scene that had never happened?

She felt as if she were in a time maze and being shuttled from the present into a past that had never been. Her logical mind rejected reincarnation as the answer. How could she be glimpsing a former life when the physical background of each experience was *identical* to the one in which she now found herself? Her bedroom, the mirror, the view of the ski slopes from the kitchen window, all the settings belonged to the here and now.

She drew her robe around her and walked over to the window. The sun had broken through dissipating clouds and was shining through the windowpane. Sunlight touched her face with a reassuring warmth. Responsive to the clear, crisp morning, she decided that she would put all her confusion on hold and get out of the house after breakfast. Exercise would clear her head and provide a welcome escape.

She showered, then dressed warmly and went downstairs and ate a quick breakfast of toast and dry cereal. Grabbing a down-filled jacket and tying a scarf on her head, she left the house by the back door. Aspen trees made a tracery of bare branches overhead as she strode up a nearby mountain slope. Moisture clinging to tall conifers fell in a watery sheen as she brushed against the soft needles. Her nostrils filled with the scent of pine, decaying leaves and moist earth. Letting her arms swing lightly at her side, she lifted her face to the sun. Several times she stopped and looked back at the house. The farther she went, the more the lines were obscured by thickening trees. Only the jagged roofline was visible with its chimneys jutting upward like claws in the bleached sky. *Claws?* Now why had that simile come to mind?

When she had climbed a good distance up the first slope, she began to hike along a natural ridge that ran in a westerly direction. Keeping herself oriented to the house, she was certain she would be able to retrace her steps easily. Granite peaks, hard and unrelenting, rose in a jagged line on the horizon like snow-covered shark's teeth. The Sawtooth Mountain Range was well named, Lynne thought, suppressing a shiver as she looked at the vaulting stark peaks.

The crisp silence was broken by the scuff of her boots as she climbed over shattered boulders that had been swept down from the rocky terrain above her. All around her sheer cliffs dropped into deep cuts in the earth. She felt infinitesimally small and insignificant. What was it Jarrett had said? *The mountains have a treachery all their own.* In spite of the warm sun, she shivered.

She hiked for about a half hour, resting from time to time as her lungs gulped oxygen-thin air. She was about to turn around and retrace her steps when her attention was caught by something unusual on a knoll just ahead. When she came closer she saw that it was a stone memorial with four wooden crosses placed in the ground around it.

She stopped in front of a brass plaque and read the names of four victims who had been buried in an avalanche on this spot, December 12, 1967. Benjamin Mitchell, age 58. Benny Mitchell, beloved grandchild, age 3. Maribelle Ashley, age 23. Sue Ann Ashley, age 26.

An exclamation of dismay broke from her lips. Like someone caught in a pounding surf, she stood there on the lonely mountainside, staring at the names. Images began to form. *No, it couldn't be!* She was suddenly filled with an inner turmoil like that at the onset of an illness. Faces became clear. A jolting recognition made her gasp, *"I have seen these people!"*

Where? When?

Slowly a memory formed in her mind. She was standing in the living room doorway, watching two young women laughing and talking on a floral green sofa; an older man was leaning against the fireplace and a child played on the floor with blocks. There was no doubt in her mind that the people she had seen were Benjamin Mitchell, his grandson and two young women, Maribelle and Sue Ann Ashley. But they're dead. Dead. Dead. All of them. How could she have imagined their presence in the house when she didn't even know they existed?

Lynne's thoughts were like fragments being swept over raging rapids, whirling, sinking and tossed in every direction. They refused to fall into any logical order. She clung to reason as defense against the betrayal of her own sanity. There had to be a rational explanation. The perceptions that had been assaulting her had to have their origins *outside* her own mind. She didn't know why or how, but the victims of a 1967 avalanche were not a figment of her imagination nor the product of a nightmare. She hadn't made them up. The people she had seen clearly had died on a mountainside and a memorial had been erected to them. *And yet, I've seen them in the house.*

She was not an advocate of psychic phenomena. Neither was she totally skeptical of spirit visitation. She'd never had any experiences with extrasensory perceptions—until now. It was as if the victims of the avalanche had pulled her out of the present and into the past with them. Even as she accepted the premise as possible, a foreboding sense of disaster engulfed her. Yesterday's nightmare came back to her—she had seen the little boy's eyes filled with terror. She remembered everything now. The way he had played with his teddy bear. His childish somersaults. The joy in his face un- til—

She stared at the white crosses. Her skin prickled. Her feet were riveted to the ground. On some weird level of awareness, these dead people were reaching out to her. Why? The cry was an anguished plea for un- derstanding but only the soft rustle of leaves blowing over the ground disturbed the silence.

She turned away slowly and began hiking back along the high ridge. With each step her numbing shock faded. It wasn't her nature to be passive, to accept be- ing acted upon. If she had become a medium for de- parted spirits there had to be a reason. Even as a child she'd demanded answers for everything. She quick- ened her steps as she felt a mounting determination to know more about those people.

She remembered seeing a cubbyhole of a newspaper office during her drive through Wolverton. A local newspaper would surely carry a detailed account of the avalanche. If not, maybe she could find someone who would tell her what had happened. The little boy's spirit pulled at her the way some of her social work cases did. She felt a need that she couldn't put aside. She had to know why she felt caught in an undertow that wouldn't let go.

Hurrying into the house, she went upstairs and grabbed her purse and keys. She had just reached the front door on her way out when a bank of warm air like a draft from a giant oven hit her back.

She turned around. Two figures were climbing the center stairs. Benjamin Mitchell held the hand of his little grandson and patiently measured his steps to those of the little boy as they mounted the stairs one by one. When they reached the landing, he lifted the boy up in his arms and carried him out of sight.

Lynne stood there for a long moment. The chill of the house returned and she was left staring at an empty staircase. *Am I mad?* Were the figures only an extension of her mind, or did they truly have a ghostly existence of their own?

By the time she reached Wolverton, a dull headache had formed behind her straining eyes. Cut into the side of the mountain, the narrow twisting road was as treacherous as she remembered. Earth fell away thousands of feet at each hairpin curve. One skid and— She pulled her lower lip in a worrying gesture. She'd take Chicago at rush hour any day.

Wolverton lay at the foot of cupping mountains. A smattering of buildings lined the two-block business district and Lynne could see scattered houses hugging the steep slopes on both sides of the has-been town.

The main road had a few cars parked along the curb and Lynne saw people ambling along the sidewalk. She drove slowly past a small grocery store and filling station, finally parking in front of an old stone building that had been remodeled at some point to house several businesses—most of which were boarded up.

A couple of men across the street stopped and gawked at her as she got out of the car. A little self-conscious under their scrutiny, she decided there was something to be said for the anonymity of Chicago's crowded streets.

The *Wolverton Weekly* had one dirty front window and a door that squeaked when she went in. A thick-shouldered man wearing a full grayish black beard was hunched over a desk covered with papers, books, pop cans, pencil holders made out of animal bone and paper plates dirty with the remains of several meals.

He didn't look around when she entered and she couldn't tell whether or not he had heard her or just didn't want to stop marking the copy in front of him. Stacks of printing litter left little floor space for maneuvering. The walls were covered with maps, calendars and cluttered bulletin boards. Beyond a row of filing cabinets, Lynne glimpsed a monstrosity of a printing press. A smell of molten metal lingered in the air.

She cleared her throat. "Good morning," she said brightly to the man's back.

He swung around in his old swivel chair. "Sorry, didn't hear you." He stuck his pencil behind a rather large ear and unwound long legs from under the chair. Somewhere in his fifties, he reminded Lynne of one of those hound dogs whose jowls droop and heavy lids cover half of their eyes. He was tall, and he had an air of unhurried movement about him. From his body language, she guessed he would be slow to anger, but once aroused, he might be as tenacious as a sharp-toothed mutt.

In her job, Lynne was used to dealing with efficient, impersonal resource people when seeking information. At her request, someone would provide the records, press clippings and any other material she wanted. This was not Chicago, she reminded herself. She was a long way from city resources, and she was at a loss as how to approach this sloe-eyed man, who was obviously making up his mind whether or not she was worthy of interrupting his work.

Lynne swallowed back her impatience. She cautioned herself not to come across as a city bureaucrat. She knew he wouldn't be impressed by her professional efficiency. On the other hand, if she started blabbing about ghosts and unexplained happenings, he'd label her a nut and that would be the end of that.

She tested a smile. His expression remained bland. "Nice sunny day after yesterday's storm."

He glanced out the window as if he hadn't noticed one way or another. Then he gave her another, long, waiting look.

"I'm staying in the Mitchell house." She thought she detected a slight flicker in his eyebrows. "Varina Mitchell and I exchanged houses for a month. I'm from Chicago. She's taking my place and I'm taking hers."

No response.

Lynne felt as if she were painstakingly laying down stepping-stones with each word, trying to coax him to follow her until she could get to the real reason for her visit. "Lynne Delevan." She stuck out her hand, challenging him to a handshake.

He hesitated for a second, then wiped his ink-stained hands on his work pants and gave her hand a man's squeeze. She managed not to wince as her birthstone ring bit into her flesh and tried to give him back as good as he gave.

He dropped his hand and said gruffly, "Griffin . . . Hugh Griffin. But everybody calls me Griff."

"I didn't expect Wolverton to have a weekly newspaper," she commented with what she hoped was the right amount of awe in her voice. Apparently that was the right approach.

"First issue was in the 1800s," he told her, thawing a little.

"And you're the editor?"

"Editor, owner, reporter and a half-dozen other hats."

"A longtime Wolverton resident?" She felt as if she were plodding through thick mud with each question.

"Yep."

"A native?"

"Nope. Lived in the next valley most of my life. Rode the bus to Wolverton's schools. My pa bought the newspaper in the twenties." He eyed her with the same kind of patience a wary mutt gives a stranger. He looked ready to chase her out the door if his big nose picked up the wrong scent.

She slowed her questions and gave him an easy smile. "I've always lived in a big city. Don't know quite what to expect, living in the middle of the Rocky Mountains." She tried a couple of other avenues of conversation without any response, so she went back to questions. "You're carrying on a family tradition, then."

He shrugged. "Took it over after I came back from Vietnam. My pa used to brag that the *Wolverton Weekly* never missed an issue."

"There must be a lot of history in this area. The Mitchell house really fascinates me."

He gave her a slow, deliberate stare. "Is that what you came in to ask me about?"

He was sharper than he looked, thought Lynne. She met his gaze straight on, challenging him to some direct answers. "Has the house always been in the Mitchell family?"

"Nope."

"Could you tell me a little bit about it? It's important." Her eye contact was steady, unblinking.

He looked away first. Then he clumsily offered her a chair as if he'd decided not to show her the door just yet. He sat back down at his desk, turning the old swivel chair in her direction. "What do you want to know?"

"Everything you can tell me."

He eyed her for a long moment before he said, "The house was built by a Denver millionaire around the turn of the century. His heirs never paid much attention to it and Benjamin Mitchell bought the house for a song when he came here from Texas in the early sixties. He'd inherited a lot of money from his first wife and Ben spent a lot of it fixing up the house and buying land. Said he wanted peace and solitude."

Lynne frowned. "Then why the Conifer Ridge Ski Resort?"

"That came later . . . after his death . . . in the late seventies. The resort never really got off the ground . . . went bankrupt after a few years. Too far from Denver to attract the ski crowd. Benjamin's second wife, Varina, lost a lot of money in the venture."

"I saw the memorial and crosses this morning when I was out hiking."

Griff shook his head. "Ben was a cross-country skier. Good one, too." He stroked his thick beard. "I never could understand why he didn't recognize the avalanche danger in that area."

"You were friends?"

His eyes darkened and he clamped his mouth in a tight line. She was curious to know what was beyond his glower but she knew she wasn't going to get any more personal revelations out of him. "I'd like to read accounts of the tragedy."

"Why?"

There was a sharpness behind those heavy-lidded eyes that belied the casual slump of his shoulders.

She chose her words carefully. "Because when you live in an old house, sometimes you can feel vibrations of the people who lived there before." That was as close as she could get to the truth without telling him that she felt herself actually becoming a part of that past.

His forehead furrowed. He glared at her as if he suspected she were playing him for some kind of dope.

Lynne tried a smile. "I'm sure you've had that feeling on occasion, haven't you? When something about a place intrigues you?"

"Might not be a good idea for a person living in an isolated house to get too interested in the past." His eyes narrowed even more. Was he making a comment or giving a warning?

Unconsciously, she gave a stubborn lift to her chin. "Maybe not…but I intend to acquaint myself with the Mitchell family as much as I can," she told him. "I'd really like to read the *Wolverton Weekly*'s coverage of the avalanche. I'm sure it's more complete than I could get in any other Colorado newspaper."

She squirmed in her chair under his blunt scrutinizing stare. His expression was unreadable and she smothered a sigh of relief when he stood up and gave a jerk of his head. "Back issues are downstairs."

She followed him. At the rear of the cramped office, he opened a door and pulled on a string attached to a naked bulb hanging over the top of narrow steps. His craggy frame was in shadow as she followed him down into a musty-smelling basement.

She saw that the floors and walls were concrete. A low ceiling of wooden beams made Lynne glance warily overhead. She hated the feeling that the old timbers could give way at any moment. Even though the place seemed to be well ventilated, her nose began to wrinkle from the dust and she gave a loud sneeze.

Griff turned on two more hanging lights, but the basement remained dim and gloomy. She could tell that some effort had been made to stack wooden boxes in order on long tables, but the labels on the boxes were too faded to read.

"Nineteen sixty-seven should be somewhere on this side of the room," said Griff as he walked to a table along a far wall. As he moved past the boxes, he stooped over and read the outside markings. Halfway down the first table, he stopped. "Here we go. What you want will be somewhere in this stack."

He pulled off the lid of one of the boxes and began handing Lynne a bundle of folded newspapers. "Light's too bad down here to go through them."

Arms loaded with weekly issues for 1967, they returned to his office. They had to search through more than half of the issues to find the ones for December. As Lynne unfolded the *Wolverton Weekly* for December 12, her stomach took a sickening plunge. She sucked in her breath as her chest tightened.

There on the front page was a photograph of a man. She stared at the picture. There was no doubt in her mind of his identity.

The photograph was of the same man she had seen a couple of hours earlier holding the hand of his grandson as they climbed the stairs.

CHAPTER FIVE

Lynne stared at the headline Avalanche Tragedy and failed to keep the paper from rattling in her hands.

"Told you it wasn't a good idea," Griff said gruffly, noting her reaction. "Blasted curiosity. Doesn't do anyone any good to dig up the past. Better to let it stay buried, if you ask me."

A silent protest caught in Lynne's throat. *What if it won't?* How could she explain that she was struggling in some kind of weird time mesh? Jarrett filled her senses with remembrance that was as real as any memories she possessed. And whether she was willing or not, the avalanche victims had intruded upon her life. She had not made them up—Benjamin's photo verified that. As she'd stood in front of the memorial crosses, the scene in the living room had flooded back into her memory. Without a doubt, pictures of the two female victims would be of the two young women she'd seen sitting on the couch, dressed in their sixties garb. And the little boy? He was relating to her on some level she didn't understand, entangling her emotions and pulling her into the past with him.

Flipping through the rest of the December issues, she failed to find any more photographs. None of little Benny Mitchell. Just his grandfather. Then she knew what was missing. She looked up at Griffin with her forehead creased in a frown. "What about the boy's parents?"

"What about them? Carole and David Mitchell. They were killed in an automobile accident when Benny was just an infant. They were living with Ben at the time. Ran off the road just a couple of miles from the house. There were rumors that Dave had been drinking. Anyway, Benjamin took the baby to raise." Griffin shook his head. "The tragedy hit Ben pretty hard . . . losing Dave, his only son, like that, and Carole, his pretty redheaded daughter-in-law. Everyone said Benjamin spoiled his grandson rotten just trying to make up for the loss of the boy's parents. He loved that kid."

I know, echoed Lynne. She had witnessed Benjamin Mitchell's protective affection as he ruffled the child's hair and carried him up the stairs.

"Until Ben married Varina, the little boy was the only thing he had in his life."

Lynne opened her mouth to ask another question, but he waved her silent. The gesture told her he'd said all he was going to. "Take the papers along. Bring them back when you're finished."

She knew he made the offer to get rid of her, but she thanked him gratefully.

He shrugged, dismissing the matter. Even before she was out the door, he was back at his desk, hunched over the copy he'd been working on when she interrupted him.

She debated about going straight back to the house but her stomach reminded her that it had been a long time since breakfast. Across the street was Nellie's Place. It was a combination café and bar—mostly bar, she discovered upon entering. An onslaught of stale beer greeted her. She couldn't tell if the decor was instant western or the real thing. Guns, spurs and a variety of horsey pictures decorated the walls, and the latest Randy Travis tune was blaring over the laughter of a few men sitting at a long bar.

She sat down at a small table near the window and picked up a worn menu offering hamburgers, steak sandwiches, beer and spirits. When the song ended, the place was abnormally quiet. She looked up and saw that the three men at the bar had stopped talking. All of them were looking at her. A bald-headed man said something out of the corner of his mouth to the woman behind the bar. Lynne heard the word "Mitchell." Whatever the barmaid said in response brought a loud guffaw from all the men.

With an arrogant swagger, the woman, who was about forty years old, came around the bar wiping her hands on an apron with Nellie embroidered on the pocket. A fuzzy mop of uncertain blond-and-gray hair sprang out from her round head. Her eyelashes dripped with black mascara. She wore a short skirt and blouse so tight that they molded every bulging roll of fat.

"Out doing a little sight-seeing? Or just taking a gander at the natives?" She put hands on her thick hips in a challenging way.

Lynne kept her voice neutral in spite of the woman's hostile tone. "I was hoping to have a little lunch."

"Is that so?" The words were a kind of snort.

"This is a café, isn't it?"

"Would you be wanting an artichoke salad or crab croquettes?" She smirked. There was a rippling of snickers at the bar. "Didn't Varina warn you that there's not a decent place to eat in Wolverton?"

The way she landed on the name Varina made Lynne decide that the woman's hostility was directed at her because she was living in the Mitchell house. Lynne decided to ignore the barbed sarcasm and said evenly, "I'll have a steak sandwich, medium rare and—"

"We're out of steak." The woman's hazel eyes were hard as stones.

"A hamburger—"

"We're out of hamburger."

"I see," said Lynne, her temper flaring. "Western hospitality at its best!"

"Sweetheart, you don't fool us none. You and that New Mexico big shot are trying to set everybody up for another skinning, ain't ya? City vultures, that's what you are. Don't give a damn about the people, how you wreck the place or anything else."

"I don't know what you're talking about. I came to Colorado for a quiet vacation."

She gave an ugly snort. "You're something else. Sweet-talking Varina out of her house."

Lynne opened her mouth to explain, then shut it again. She could tell from the expressions of the woman and the men at the bar that they had already closed their minds against her. Why was she the enemy? She doubted if anyone would have lifted a finger if she'd been lying on the floor bleeding to death.

She picked up her purse and stood up.

"Bye, honey. Have a nice day." Raucous laughter followed Lynne outside.

She fought a sick feeling in the pit of her stomach as she drove back to the house. Something ugly curled around her. Even at midday, deep shadows from the surrounding peaks fell upon the landscape, making the house a dark specter through the trees as she rounded the last curve in the road.

The house stood flanked by tall ponderosa pines. Waiting. Calling to her in the same way it had in the photo Varina had sent. Why had she felt such an overwhelming affinity the first time she had looked at the picture? Was she a pawn in some kind of psychic chess game? She gave a self-mocking laugh. What nonsense! The sensible thing to do was pack her bags and leave. She'd manage somehow for a month until her condo was vacant again. Once away form the house…and Jarrett— Why lie to herself? She couldn't dismiss the deep feelings he aroused in her. Something held her to the house—and to him. Like someone surrendering to unseen forces, she climbed out of the car and went inside.

She heated a pot of soup before she spread the newspapers out on the kitchen table and began to read. The accounts were written in a precise, journalistic style. No sentimental accolades. Two sisters, Maribelle and Sue Ann Ashley, had been houseguests of

Benjamin Mitchell and his second wife, Varina, who were raising Ben's orphaned three-year-old grandson. On the day of the tragedy, all of the adults, except Varina, were hiking in snowshoes along a mountain ridge. The child was riding in a sled pulled by his grandfather when an avalanche roared down the mountainside, burying the victims under a mass of rocks and snow. Varina returned from a trip to Denver to find rescuers searching with dogs and long poles for the victims. Their bodies were never recovered but one of Ben's snowshoes, a lady's stocking cap and a little red wagon had been swept to the surface in the rolling mass.

Lynne rested her head in her hands. She knew more about the people from her own experience than from these sterile newspaper accounts. Benjamin's tenderness and love had come through clearly as she watched him carry the boy in his arms. His grandson had loved him, too. There had been confidence and trust in the little hand holding that of his grandfather. And when she had seen the two young women, they had been full of laughter and chatter. Even now she could picture them sitting on the sofa in their colorful granny dresses, their music from the record player swirling around them.

Lynne raised her head from her hands and leaned back in the kitchen chair. The present and the past were somehow meshed together. *And I'm being pulled back and forth in a time warp.* Even as she accepted the impossible, danger like a cold blast hit the back of her neck.

Her hands gripped the table. She turned her head. The little boy stood in the doorway. He was crying and clutching a teddy bear that had one ear torn from it. His little features were twisted with anguish.

Struggling against an unseen menace, she tried to reach him. He turned and fled down the hall ahead of her. "Benny... Benny!" She saw him clearly as he reached the front door. Then it swung open and a pair of firm arms went around Lynne, blocking her way.

"Lynne, for heaven's sake, what's going on?"

A spate of colors revolved in a whirlpool in front of her eyes. "Jarrett?" She stared at his face.

"You haven't forgotten me in one day, have you?" Concern deepened the lines in his face as he kept steadying hands on her.

She leaned into him and clung to him as if life were draining away with every breath. She began sobbing.

"Lynne, snap out of it!" He held her tightly, his hands moving in soothing reassurance on her back. "It's all right... it's all right."

The roar in her ears faded. Warmth began to seep back into her limbs. Her head cleared. She pulled back, avoiding direct contact with his eyes.

Gently, he led into the living room and eased her down on the sofa. Sitting beside her, he brushed back hair from her cheeks and touched his hand to her forehead as if seeking a temperature. Muscles flickered in his deeply tanned cheeks.

After a moment, her breathing returned to normal. She felt utterly foolish. Now that all tremors had passed, she couldn't believe she had behaved in such an irrational manner. Throwing her arms around him, embracing him with such fearful passion. He must think her utterly demented.

"Tell me what happened," he ordered.

She searched his face. His expression was solemn. His eyes were clear and probing. She felt no lingering sense that she had known him beyond the day before yesterday. He was a stranger, perplexed by her behavior and wanting to hear a rational explanation for the way she had barreled into his arms as he opened the door.

A rational explanation, an inner voice mocked. How would he react if she told him she'd been intent on communicating with a sobbing little boy who had died twenty-five years ago? That she had felt danger swirling around him and she'd been determined to protect him. She could imagine Jarrett's withdrawal, his guarded response and perhaps even a glint of pity in his eyes.

She swallowed hard. Turning her gaze from his face, she gave a nervous swipe to hair drifting forward on her face. The strands were moist with perspiration. She searched for some way to begin—and failed. How could she explain something she didn't understand herself?

He waited.

She lifted her chin. "What are you doing here so early?" She needed time to collect herself emotionally. Somehow she had to get things back on an even keel. The panicked sensation was fading; she felt self-control returning. "It's only a little past noon." She was relieved to hear her voice quite normal.

"I couldn't set up a business meeting in White Springs until tomorrow morning, so I decided to come back."

"I didn't expect you until evening." And then she added rather archly, "If at all."

He grinned, as if relieved. "Well, your temper is still firing on all cylinders, I see. Now, what's going on here?"

She offered him a glib line. "I...I thought I heard someone in the house. When I opened the door you startled me."

"You didn't open the door, *I* did. And you looked at me as if you'd never seen me before," he countered. "Besides, I heard you calling in a loud voice as I mounted the front steps."

I was calling to a distraught little boy named Benny to wait for me. She moistened her lips. "You must have heard me asking 'Is anybody there?'"

He stared at her, his intense blue eyes peeling away the thin veneer of composure that she was struggling to maintain. As if he feared she were about to fall off some dark emotional edge, his tone changed. "Well, lady, what you need is a drink, and I just happen to have a couple of bottles of wine, brandy and a six-pack of beer in the car. We'll have ourselves a nice relaxed time in front of the fire, then you can tell me what's been happening while I was gone."

He gave her a reassuring smile. He was handling her warily, as if she were about to come apart in his hands.

If she told him about the people in the house, the ones who'd been killed in the avalanche, he'd never believe that her experiences were anything but hallucinatory. Even if she protested that she had seen the dead people before she had even learned of their existence, he would try to find some logical explanation, the way she had in the beginning. And he was a part of that weird shift in time. She had memories of him that were more real than those of her childhood. She couldn't explain it—not to herself, not to him.

They sat on the couch in the library. She sipped a glass of rose wine and he had a can of beer. He offered some pistachio nuts. "My favorite snack," he said.

I know. Her lip quivered. *You always eat nuts with your beer... and pistachios are your favorite.* She cleared her throat. "Thank you," she said in an even tone. She had to remind herself that he was a stranger, not the passionate lover she had seen so vividly in the bedroom mirror.

Jarrett settled back beside her on the couch, stretching his long legs out in front of a crackling fire. With precision, he cracked the nuts and jetted the shells into the fireplace. Then he grinned at her like a little boy wanting approval for his marksmanship.

She couldn't help but laugh at him.

"That's better." He nodded with approval. "I like it when your eyes turn a misty blue... and when your lips curve ever so softly."

Steady, girl, she cautioned, stiffening against being swept into another emotional whirlpool.

He began to talk about his meeting with the county commissioners. She relaxed, feeling more and more comfortable as they sat there sipping their drinks.

A contest emerged as they spit nutshells into the fire. The challenge was to see who could send the shells the farthest. Laughing, Lynne did her best but finally conceded defeat when the hearth was covered with shells.

"The winner gets a kiss." Before she could protest, Jarrett claimed his prize. His lips touched hers, sending remembered warmth through her, and her mouth instinctively opened to deepen the kiss. The fiery heat of her breath mingled with his as the familiar caressing of his tongue changed her breath to a short gasp.

He raised his head from the devastating kiss, his eyes wide and flashing with sudden surprise at the invitation her clinging embrace had offered.

Realizing that she had unwittingly sent him the wrong message, she felt the heat of embarrassment rising in her cheeks. She pulled away, keeping her eyes averted from his as she took a generous sip of her drink.

After a moment, he said in a companionable tone, "You haven't told me what you did today."

She took a deep breath to keep her tone casual. "I went to Wolverton."

"Not much of a place, is it?"

She frowned, remembering the unpleasant scene in the café. "I tried to have lunch at Nellie's Place, but the animosity was thick enough to cut. I had the feeling the townspeople were ready to lynch Varina and anyone slightly connected with her. They accused me and 'that New Mexico big shot' of setting them up for another skinning."

Jarrett seemed to try for a smile but couldn't quite manage it. "Can't say that I blame them for having a bad taste in their mouth. From what I learned, Varina Mitchell made about every mistake in the book trying to operate a ski resort. She put up most of the money, obtained a U.S. Forestry Service permit in *her* name instead of the corporation, as required. When the permit ran out, she failed to come up with a $45,000 bond for a new one. The Feds were about to shut her down when the whole thing went into bankruptcy." He shook his head. "I'm afraid the people around here thought they were into another gold rush, but the Conifer Ridge Ski Resort turned out to be a bust. And they blame Varina Mitchell for it."

"Why would anyone be interested in investing money in it now?"

"Because with the right kind of money and management the area could be developed into a profitable resort. Some problems would have be solved—like ready transportation. I don't know how Varina expected people to get here. She didn't set up any commuter flights out of Denver to White Springs, and no shuttle bus service to the ski area. There weren't any condo accommodations close by. Even though Wolverton business people spent a lot of money renovating some buildings in town, they lost their shirts when nobody came. It's not surprising they're ready to resist any new 'let's put Wolverton on the map' schemes.''

Jarrett fell silent and she could tell his thoughts had sped away to business. She realized with a start that he had reached out and taken her hand as they talked. His thumb lightly caressed the soft cleft in her hand in an unconscious gesture. Her mind faltered as she tried to understand how he could be an enigma to her on one level, while on another she knew him with an intimacy that defied all logic.

She withdrew her hand and turned toward him. ''I took a hike this morning and found a memorial to four people killed in an avalanche in 1967.''

He nodded. ''Varina's husband and grandson... according to some background information we have on her,'' said Jarrett readily. ''Who were the other two?''

''Sisters. Maribelle and Sue Ann Ashley. Guests of the Mitchell's, according to a newspaper account. That's why I went to Wolverton. The editor let me bring home some old papers about the avalanche.''

His eyes darkened. ''Why would you want to do that?''

''I was ... curious.'' Lynne finished her wine and set the glass on a side table. Her hand trembled slightly and she hoped he didn't notice. She licked her lips. *I have seen the victims ... here in the house.* The words formed but they never passed her lips.

''I guess such tragedies are not unusual in the high country,'' he said, studying her expression.

"No, I guess not."

"Is that why you're strung out? Are you afraid that the house is going to get buried under an avalanche when it starts snowing?"

The idea was so ridiculous she laughed softly. "I swear the thought never crossed my mind."

"Then what is it about the house that sends shivers up your back?"

Her mirth faded and she looked away.

"Tell me. What made you greet me in such a frantic way?"

She could hear herself saying, *The little boy was in danger. He reached out to me and I wanted to protect him.* His puzzled response. *What little boy?* She'd answer, *Benny Mitchell.* The look he'd give her would be tightly controlled but the recoil would be there. *The boy's dead,* he would say in that measured voice of his. And there would be pity in his eyes.

Her hands tensed in her lap. She remained silent.

"Lynne." He cupped her chin and forced her to look into his arresting eyes. "Were you having another dream? Were you sleepwalking by any chance?"

"Sleepwalking?" she echoed. "Why would you think that?"

"I don't know. Just the way you acted. Your eyes . . . your expression. Like somebody in a trance."

"I wasn't sleeping. I was fully awake."

His hand slipped from her chin and he let his fingertips trace the sweet line of her cheek and the bowed curves of her full lips. For a long moment he just looked at her. She knew then that the physical attraction was real ... born of the present ... and that frightened her even more because she had already recognized it as a memory.

CHAPTER SIX

That night, dinner was everything Jarrett had promised. Tender veal cutlets smothered in a golden Dijon mustard gravy and topped with chopped mushrooms, surrounded by buttered parsley potatoes and glazed carrots. Bakery rolls warmed in the oven glistened with real butter, and for dessert he offered her a slice of a German chocolate cake, oozing with nuts, coconut and brown sugar topping.

He insisted on eating in the dining room. They found several damask tableclothes and napkins in one of the buffets, and despite Lynne's qualms about making themselves too much at home, Jarrett insisted on lighting white candles in a silver candelabra.

He had shooed her out of the kitchen while he prepared the food, so she took a leisurely bath in the clawfooted tub. She'd brought some fragrant bubble bath, and even though the water was only tepid, a brisk rubbing brought a glow to her skin and a sheen to her hair. He was making such a production out of the dinner, she decided to rise to the occasion by wearing a long quilted skirt of rainbow colors and a black jersey blouse with matching appliqué flowers. As she stood in front of the mirror and slipped on small gold earrings, the wallpaper reflected in the mirror seemed to change into a spriggy lavender pattern, summer vines loaded with tiny flowers. She swung around, her eyes rounded and expectant. Her hands were tightly clenched at her side. She was rigid. Waiting. But nothing happened. Nothing had changed. The walls were still papered in the gaudy cabbage rose pattern. No lavender wallpaper. The whispered past like a faint breeze touched her face and then disappeared.

She hurried from the room.

Jarrett gave her an appreciative grin as he seated her in a high-backed chair at one end of the table.

"Nice perfume."

She flushed, foolishly pleased that she'd dressed for a date. He brought in their plates, sat down in a chair on her left and poured their wine.

In the midst of old-fashioned elegance, Lynne visualized a family gathering around the table. China and silverware graced the damask cloth, the same light shone overhead with its Tiffany shade hanging low, and the sideboards were loaded with silver tureens and steaming dishes. Her chest suddenly tightened as she looked around the table at each empty chair, unconsciously steeling herself for that sudden slip of time gears.

"What's the matter?" Jarrett put down his fork and followed her gaze around the empty room. "Why did you go tense all of a sudden? What is it? You seem to be looking for something...or someone?"

How could she explain to him that in some realm of consciousness, she might at any moment slip back in time and experience a dinner party that took place years ago in this very room? What rational person would believe it? Certainly not this self-assured, extremely competent man who already must wonder if she was functioning on all cylinders. He'd probably be kind enough, listen intently and try to understand, but in the end he'd say that she was letting her imagination run rampant. But she wasn't! She wasn't just dreaming these incidents—she was experiencing them!

"Now you're glaring at me as if you're about to plunge that fork into my heart."

She felt utterly foolish. She was *here,* in the *present.* The man sitting beside her was of the moment. He filled her senses, causing undefinable emotions to flicker within her. Deep, possessive longings smoldered with latent heat. As she looked at him, arresting shadows played upon his face, highlighting the strong planes of his brow and cheeks and deepening the dark clarity of his eyes. Without saying anything, he had the power to make her feel wonderfully feminine and desirable. Her heartbeat quickened and she gave him an apologetic smile. "Sorry."

He searched her face and then gave her a wry grin. "Listen, if you don't like the food, just say so and I'll open a can of beans."

She laughed. "The food is wonderful…and so is the company," she assured him.

He reached over and closed his fingers around hers. He lifted her hand and she felt the warmth of his breath on her skin as he placed a kiss in her palm. Then he released her hand gently as if it held something precious.

She wanted to say something light and facetious, but she couldn't. He was a practiced dinner partner and she suspected that he entertained all his ladies in such a romantic fashion. He was skilled in the art of seduction and there was a sensuous side to him that was like a spell. His touch, his eyes and softly smiling lips lured her into a web of desire.

As if aware of her inner turmoil, he artfully led the conversation into a discussion of restaurants and gourmet chefs. They compared likes and dislikes. None of his preferences surprised her.

She described her favorite restaurant, a tiny hole-in-the-wall Italian place whose menu was simple but perfectly prepared and simply served.

"Is that where your favorite dates take you?"

"That's where *I* take *them*," she countered with a sexist's smile. "*I* don't prepare company meals at home."

He chuckled. "Maybe you need a good teacher... like me?"

"Do you come with recommendations?"

"The very best... all kinds, in fact." His eyes promised much more than sharing recipes.

She let out a shaky breath. "I believe you."

Candlelight flickered in the depths of his eyes and she looked away quickly, fearful that she would give in to the irresistible pull that would have her in his arms before she could take another breath.

"I'll help do the kitchen cleanup," she offered when they had finished dessert.

"No, you won't. The cook cleans up after himself. I don't want you counting how many pans I dirtied. My mother used to put her hand over her mouth when she'd see the kitchen after I'd fixed a meal." He laughed. "I never could get the hang of economy when it came to pots and pans. She was a good sport, though. Let me do my worst and was ready to eat my failures as well as my successes. I think she's glad I have my own place. When I invite her and Dad over for a meal, she walks out of my apartment without ever looking in the kitchen."

"She sounds great. My mother..." Lynne hesitated. "Well, let's just say she preferred to have a place for everything and—"

"Everything in its place," he finished. "Pretty hard on kids. I guess I was lucky."

"Yes," she said, and then felt guilty. "But my mother was a single parent at a time when such a status was not socially acceptable. I guess that's one of the reasons I went into social work...to try to help children who came from broken homes."

"I bet every kid loves you for it," he said softly. "You're probably more dedicated than is good for you."

"That's what my friend Dixie says." She smiled. "You'd like Dixie." Lynne made up her mind at that moment to tell her friend about Jarrett the next time she called.

"Is your father still alive?"

She shook her head. "My mother was widowed when I was three. Fortunately, we lived close to my

grandfather. He was the greatest." Her eyes softened.
"I was lucky to have him as a kind of father figure.
He..." Her voice trailed off. She was about to say that,
in a way, Benjamin Mitchell reminded her of her own
grandfather. The realization took her by surprise.
*Maybe that's why I'm sensitive to seeing him and his
grandson. I've felt the same kind of love they have for
each other.*

Jarrett waved a hand in front of her face. "Come
back...come back...wherever you are," he coaxed in
a light singsong voice.

She returned his grin. "Sorry."

"You were telling me about your grandfather."

"He...we...had a special rapport," she said halt-
ingly, trying to explain. "When he was dying, my
mother called me at college and I made reservations on
the next flight to go home. The weather was bad in
Chicago—as it always is in January—and the plane
developed trouble with its landing gear. We circled the
airport for an eternity that night and the attendants
prepared us for an emergency landing. On the way
down, my heart was stuck in my throat, and suddenly
I felt my grandfather sitting beside me. He seemed to
be reassuring me the way he had so many times when I
came to him with my fears. We landed safely. But when
I got to the hospital, I found out he had died while my
plane was in the air." Lynne's lips trembled slightly as
she said, "I think his spirit was with me for that brief
moment when I needed him."

Jarrett gently eased back a lock of hair that had
fallen on her forehead. His touch was reassuring but

she knew from his expression that he discounted the incident as wishful thinking. She was glad she hadn't told him about the warm feelings she had toward the ghostly little boy and his grandfather.

At his insistence, they took their coffee into the living room. Jarrett put a Johnny Mathis classic on the stereo and began humming along.

Lynne felt a foolish smile on her own lips as he set her coffee cup down on an end table and pulled her to her feet.

"Hmm, nice," he breathed, putting his cheek against hers as they danced to the romantic music. He held her with a masculine domination, keeping his hand firmly on her back, melting her length against his. With every step, the tantalizing brush of his legs brought a spiral of sensation that was both exquisite and torturing. She tried to control her quickened breathing, to still the quivering ache of desire and deny a mounting impulse to raise her lips to his.

As Johnny Mathis sang about love, a warning sounded as the lyrics echoed in her head. *Love?* She'd always been reasonable about falling in love. Kept her heart well cushioned against the kind of emotional upheaval she was feeling in this man's arms. She scarcely knew him. It was the bewildering memories she'd entertained about him that had clouded her judgment. He was probably just thinking of her as a convenient conquest.

"What's the matter?" He was startled by the way she had gone cold in his arms, pulling away before the last measure of the song had finished.

"I'm really very tired. I think I'd better call it a day."
She had herself in hand now that she was out of his
arms. "I'll do breakfast in the morning. But don't expect anything fancy," she warned, at the same time
wondering if she could remember the recipe for some
delicious oat bran muffins she had made last Christ-
mas.

"Are you sure you won't have a nightcap? A spot of
brandy?"

"No thanks. My head's light from the dinner wine,"
she said airily. *And other things.*

He walked with her to the bottom of the stairs. She
quickly mounted three of them before she turned
around, out of his reach. "See you in the morning."
She didn't trust herself with a good-night kiss—how-
ever casual.

He gave her a languid, slightly amused smile. "Sweet
dreams."

Lynne sat on the edge of her bed, trying to deny the
need to fulfill the fantasies that tortured her as memories. All evening she had plied Jarrett with questions,
trying to understand why he seemed familiar to her.
Nothing in his background or environment touched
any familiar chord. She had failed to find one rational
reason why he appeared to her in mental flashes like
memories. How could she maintain a friendly distance from this man when everything about him drew
her to him? What would happen if she let down the
barriers and surrendered? Would the spell he'd put on
her disappear and leave her with a loneliness that would
haunt her the rest of her life?

She hugged herself against the chill of the room. *Who are you, Jarrett? Why does your presence torture me with such longing?* Acute loneliness suddenly drove away all the warmth and companionship of the evening. Shivering, she made ready for bed.

The day's events whirled like a kaleidoscope behind her closed eyes as she lay there—the morning's walk with its dramatic discovery, Griff's newspaper office and Nellie and her sneering friends. Going over everything that had happened, she wondered why the bearded editor had tried to discourage her interest in the Mitchell house? Did he have something to hide? He'd let her take the papers, but with a warning. Maybe he—

She lost the thought. If she'd been asleep, the light footsteps on the stairs would have gone unnoticed. She stiffened. Jarrett? Was he coming to her room? Her heartbeat suddenly lurched into rapid pounding. She would send him away. She would. No, she'd pretend to be asleep, that's what she'd do. But what if he just opened the door and walked in? Lynne tried to ready herself as his footsteps approached her door.

It was a long moment before she realized that the person had gone past her bedroom. The steps grew faint as they continued down the hall. It had to be Jarrett. Where was he going? What was he doing walking down the second-floor hall? A door squeaked. Muffled footsteps on the attic stairs. She sat up. Why was he going up to the attic?

She brushed a hand across her eyes. Was she living in the past again? Her ears strained for the sound of voices, laughter or music. Silence. She turned on the bed light. Her robe lay on the foot of the bed, the paperback book she had started to read waited on the bedside table. Everything was of the present.

She took a deep breath. *All right, if I'm experiencing the moment as it is happening, what in blazes is Jarrett Taylor up to?* Why would he be slipping up to the attic in such a furtive way? She could hear the boards creaking with his weight overhead. He must be walking from one end to the other.

She grabbed her blue corduroy robe, tied the belt with an impatient jerk and pushed her feet into the warm fleece-lined bedroom slippers. She remembered that he had wanted to go up to the attic when they were touring the house. What was he after?

She slipped out into the hall. A bright light spilled through the doorway from the bedroom beyond hers. She wavered, put her hand out against the wall to keep her balance. Drawn by an invisible magnet, she walked slowly forward until she stood in the radius of lucent light. As a pink satin gown and robe fell around her slippered feet, she knew she was outside a memory and yet a part of it.

The remembered sweet scent of baby powder touched her nostrils as the room came into focus. A nursery. Two bassinets stood in the center of the room, one covered in pink ruffled satin, the other in blue eyelet. She could see the fluttering of small arms and hear the soft sounds of infant murmurings. Her gaze was drawn to a rocking chair placed by the window. A shadowy figure moved it back and forth in slow, measured rhythm. As Lynne's eyes fixed upon it, she had the weird sensation that *she* was the person sitting there, her breasts heavy with milk and her body ripe with impending childbirth.

The bright light slowly dimmed. Her vision narrowed. All sound faded away, and the scene that had formed in her mind was sucked away into some deep recess of her awareness as if it had never been. When her vision cleared, she was staring into the shadowy guest bedroom with Early American decor and maple bedroom furniture. She leaned against the door frame, fighting the shudders that wracked her body.

A moment later, Jarrett's anxious voice came over her shoulder and his firm hands turned her around. "What is it? You look ready to faint. What's the matter?" He looked past her into the ordinary bedroom. "What's there? What frightened you?"

She leaned into him, drawing reassurance from the undisputed reality of his presence. His heartbeat was steady and strong as he pulled her close. She welcomed the strength of his hands pressed firmly against her back. Nothing about him was an illusion. At the moment he was an anchor in reality, a fixed point in a bizarre stream of consciousness that had her plunging in and out of experiences that had never happened. A single frustrated tear squeezed from her eyes and coursed down her cheek.

"Don't cry," he said gently as she shivered in his embrace. "It's all right. I'm here."

Her mind refused to deliver an image of what she'd seen as she stood there, trembling. Like a negative turning black, the memory was lost forever in the depths of her subconscious. She raised her head and stared at him. In the dimly lighted hall, his face was in shadow. By any measurement of logic, she should be afraid of this man. He was a stranger who had just walked into her life and yet in some intangible way had been a part of her existence forever. Something stronger than rational thought made her accept the inevitable. She loved him. She always had.

He brushed away her tear and laid his cheek against hers, holding her tightly. For a long moment neither of them moved, the length of their bodies pressed together. A rising flow of warmth invaded the clammy chill in her limbs. He held her body firmly against his until the tremors eased and her confusion ebbed like a slowly retreating tide. Gradually she relaxed, her body becoming supple in his embrace. He cupped her face with his hand and searched her eyes.

"All right now?" he murmured.

She nodded.

He put his arm around her waist and walked her back to her room. In some unfathomable way there was no reality beyond that which he brought to her. He anchored her to the present . . . and to the past. She wanted to be in his arms and lose herself in a strange renewing of the pleasure that she knew lay within his embrace. "I . . . I don't want you to go."

In the dim light of the hall, she saw a shadow pass over his face as if he struggled with some uneasiness of his own. His carefully controlled responses hinted at some private conflict; she could sense a darkness in him that he kept hidden.

"Is there someone else?" she asked hoarsely.

The tension eased around his mouth. "No. There's no one."

Even though a warning quivered in the edges of her mind, she whispered, "Please stay."

His voice was husky. "Are you sure?"

She was bewildered by her emotions and desire for this man who seemed so familiar, and yet was a stranger to her. There was nothing rational about the way she felt, but she *was* sure that she wanted him to stay.

For an answer she raised her face to his. He tightened his embrace and kissed her. Gentle yet demanding, his mouth worked hers, shaping her lips with his questing tongue until the heat and flame of his kiss obliterated all thought. One hand cupped the back of her head and the other slowly and deliberately loosened the belt on her robe. His probing gaze searched her face as if waiting for a flicker of resistance.

She only smiled, raised her hand and traced his cheek. His flesh was hot beneath her touch. Last night a similar experience had befuddled her senses and she had been left trembling. But tonight her perceptions were startlingly clear.

He drew her to the bed, slipped the gown from her flushed body. When he had shed his clothes, he eased under the covers beside her. As they lay together, the truth was vivid and indisputable—on some level of experience they had made love many times. She knew the planes and curves of his masculine strength and had felt his tender exploring touch as they experienced the wonder of fulfilling desire.

"You are so beautiful," he murmured. He moved the hand that had been stroking her cheek to the sweet softness of her neck, and then to the budding nipples of her smooth breasts, his fingertip lightly coaxing them into responding hardness. Every touch, caress and kiss fired an undeniable cue to forgotten memories.

Her body remembered even if her mind could not. She sighed as she breathed in his scent, and a tiny shiver of mounting desire built into a trembling that brought a soft moan to her lips.

He muffled her husky cries with kisses and a questing tongue that teased her mouth into willing submission. With tantalizing gentleness he explored the firm swell of her breasts and the rounded smoothness of her hips and thighs. Every kiss and caress increased the rising crescendo of their passion. And when they came together, the measured thrusts of his body flamed a bursting delight within her. His husky whispering was a counterpoint to her own cries, trapped in a breathless ecstasy.

When their passion was spent, Lynne nestled contentedly into the warm curve of his arm and shoulder. One of her hands rested upon his chest, rising and falling with the rhythmic beating of his heart. No dreams taunted her peaceful slumber as she slept warm and contented in his arms.

* * *

In the morning, she awakened slowly in a haze of confused thoughts and feelings. All tension was gone from her body. She stirred under the covers and opened her languid eyes to morning light. It took her a long moment to realize that she was alone in the bed and that an insidious chill had invaded the room.

CHAPTER SEVEN

Lynne showered, then dressed quickly in jeans and sweatshirt and hurried downstairs. No smell of coffee or any sign of breakfast in the kitchen—a sharp contrast to the morning before, when Jarrett had been waiting for her.

She stood for a moment in the middle of the room, hugging herself against the cold—and something else her mind refused to define. He hadn't told her why he had gone up to the attic in the middle of the night. A knot lodged in her throat as she walked down the back hall and knocked on his closed door.

"Jarrett?"

Silence answered her rather strained call. Steeling herself, she turned the knob and let the door swing open. Papers were strewn on the bed. Haste was evident in objects tumbled on the night table and chest of drawers. His suitcase was still there and a pile of dirty clothes were in a heap. The room was beautifully messy.

He hadn't left.

She leaned up against the door frame. He must have overslept and had to make a mad dash not to be late for the appointment he had that morning in White Springs. Not trusting her own perceptions about what had happened last night, she had expected the room to be empty, a mockery to the shared passion that had sent her senses reeling.

A flood of unbelievable joy went through her, followed by a sense of utter dismay. What on earth was happening to her? If someone had told her she'd be behaving this way with a man she barely knew, she would have been horrified. She couldn't believe that she'd been so devastated this morning when she had found Jarrett had left. What, really, did she know about him? Everything he said about himself might be the truth, or none of it. She sensed he was holding something back. His reason for coming to the area seemed legitimate, but still... In spite of what had happened between them, he might have only the most superficial of feelings for her, a pointed contrast to the intense emotions he aroused in her. No, she wouldn't believe that. He had made love to her as if nothing so wonderful had happened before. She laughed aloud. "He's real. And he's coming back."

Her steps were light as she fixed a full breakfast instead of her usual coffee and toast. A bright sun shining through the kitchen window matched her cheery mood. It was only ten o'clock when she finished the kitchen cleanup. A nervous twisting in her stomach reminded her that she had the whole day to get through before he came back. A quiver of apprehension overtook her but she quickly pushed it away. Better that she anchor herself in the moment, concentrate on doing housekeeping, washing clothes and other mundane chores, she told herself firmly.

Her tasks went quickly and she finished all her chores by noon. She ate a sandwich and cup of soup and decided on a brisk walk to use up some of her energy—and make the time go faster until Jarrett got back.

Leaving the house, she decided not to go as far as the memorial crosses. Her mood was not right for such somber reminders. She felt vibrantly alive. *I won't look beyond today.* Like someone inhaling heady perfume, she filled her nostrils with the scent of pine and clean earth as she set out on a brisk climb up the slope she had called Buttermilk Run. Her skin tingled and her lips and cheeks grew rosy in the crisp air.

She stopped several times to catch her breath. The only sounds that disturbed the silence were a raucous bird cawing at her and the crackling of deadfall under her boots. When her legs told her she'd climbed far enough, she rested a few minutes on a fallen log and viewed the narrow valley below.

For a brief instant her mouth went dry and she tensed as her gaze traveled over the landscape. Then she relaxed with a weak chuckle. Her perceptions had not swung off in any weird direction. Even though she could imagine the whole area covered with snow, skiers sailing down the white trails and wafts of smoke coming from chimneys, the slopes remained barren with dry leaves and the abandoned buildings were silent. No tricks of the mind, no sense of familiarity overtook her. A lingering impression that she had once skied these slopes was absurd. She had only been two or three years old when the Conifer Ridge Ski Resort was in operation. Daydreaming must have accounted for the view she had seen from the kitchen window.

She started back down the slope, letting her eyes travel along the base of the small valley where the abandoned buildings clustered together. Curious, she turned her steps in that direction. She made her way carefully around piles of stone, wood and mortar and paused to read a couple of faded signs that identified a ski shop and alpine store.

Several small buildings leaned together as if braced against the wind, but most of them were nothing more than heaps of gray boards. The few structures left standing looked ready to collapse with the next gust of wind and she knew better than to get too close. Only a forsaken lodge stood partially intact with its windows gone and steep roof sagging in the middle. As Lynne's gaze roved over its forlorn exterior, her eyes did a double take. She stiffened. What was that? She thought she saw a fleeting movement in one of the sagging doorways.

She took a few steps forward and then stopped. The only sound in the eerie silence was the wind passing through the dilapidated building with a high-pitched wail. She gave herself a mental shake. A trick of light must have fooled her into thinking she'd seen something moving inside.

She turned away. Ghost towns must be like this, she thought. Empty. Dead. And yet strangely filled with poignant reminders of life and people. Suddenly the silence was broken. A rumble like far-off thunder grew louder and louder. She heard a crash of falling timbers inside the old lodge. She swung around.

Dust poured out of every opening. Lynne covered her mouth and stepped back. A second round of rumbling shook the outer walls. The whole roof was going to go! Even standing out in the open she was at risk if any of the outside walls fell in her direction. She turned to run—

The man was right behind her, half-hidden in the shadow of a pile of debris.

Lynne's mouth opened in a soundless scream. Her knees buckled. He reached forward and grabbed her. A mass of black hair swirled in front of her eyes. She clawed at it with her nails before she recognized the face under the beard.

"Let go, damn you." Anger flashed hotly in his heavy-lidded eyes. "What the hell? You didn't have to attack me like a wild animal."

She uncurled her fingers from Griff's beard. He dropped his huge hands from her shoulders. Fright had taken away her breath. She gasped, "And you didn't have to sneak around and frighten me half to death."

"I wasn't sneaking around...as you put it. Just having a look." He gave her a cool, challenging stare. "What were you doing?"

His black eyebrows were matted in an accusing way. What business was it of his? "The same," she snapped.

"You could have got yourself killed," he lashed out.

"Were you in the old lodge earlier?" she demanded.

"I have more sense than that," he growled.

"I thought I saw someone . . . before it collapsed."

He gave her a sardonic smile. "A ghost, perhaps?"

She met his gaze steadily. "Does the Mitchell house have the reputation of being haunted, by any chance?"

He seemed to find the question amusing. "You don't reckon Varina would have lived here all these years by herself if it was, do you?"

A good question, thought Lynne.

They had started walking back toward the house. "I'm sorry if I startled you," he said gruffly. "Your visit yesterday reminded me of a few things. Thought I'd just refresh my memory a little." He lifted his eyes to the old house with its dark windows looking down at them. "Used to come up here quite often."

"In the sixties?" she heard herself ask. She guessed he'd have been twenty-five or thirty years old about then. He rubbed his chin. She saw a dribble of blood had collected on his beard where she'd scratched him.

"I'm sorry," she said.

"Haven't met up with a wildcat for a long time." He almost smiled.

"Come on up to the house. You can wash off. Then you can look around. Reminisce."

"About the good old days?"

"Were they?" she asked bluntly. Her curiosity about him and his connection with the Mitchell family was mounting.

He shrugged. She wondered what thoughts suddenly caused the flintlike hardness in his eyes. She tried to read his expression when they entered the house, and couldn't. His craggy face remained like granite as he

looked around the foyer, glanced up the staircase and
then followed her down the hall. As they passed the
locked double doors, she asked impulsively, "What
room is that?"

"Benjamin's game room," he answered readily.

"I wonder why it's locked."

He walked over to the doors and reached up on the
top of the door frame, ran his fingers along the ledge
and brought down a tarnished brass key.

"Ben always kept it there," he said, slipping it in the
lock. He opened the door and made a gesture for her
to go in first.

She hesitated. Maybe she shouldn't.

Griff watched her, a challenge in his eyes. She
walked past him into the darkened room. Griff gave a
flip of the light switch but nothing happened. The only
illumination came from a pair of French doors with
half-drawn shades.

A large pool table in the middle of the room seemed
to be the only piece of furniture. A host of eyes
watched her as she moved forward into the room,
sending a prickling across the nape of her neck. She
tipped her head up and met the glassy gaze of animal
eyes looking down at her.

She lowered her eyes and glanced around the dusky
room. She couldn't see anything that accounted for the
door being locked—until she turned back to Griff.

Her breath caught. The bearded man stood facing
her with a hunting rifle in his hand. Behind him on the
wall was a mounted rack filled with an assortment of

guns. He lifted the rifle and peered down its sight, aiming at some point that seemed frightfully close.

She kept the panic out of her voice as she asked, "Is it loaded?"

For a moment he didn't act as if he'd heard her. Then he lowered the gun, opened the barrel and took out a shell. "Not now." He turned around and put the gun back on the rack.

Strength flowed back into her knees. The room with its mounted animal heads and Griff's readiness with the gun had left her more shaken than she would have liked to admit. "We'd better lock up again," she told him as she walked past him and out the door. "I'll get a washcloth for your face."

He followed her into the kitchen. The old newspapers were lying on the table and he asked, "Did you satisfy your curiosity?"

"I found the accounts pretty skimpy," she said honestly. "There wasn't anything about the Ashley sisters except their names. Did you know them?"

Griff wiped his face and handed her back the cloth. "Nope. Didn't even know they were visiting until after the avalanche."

Lynne searched his homely face. Was he lying? She couldn't tell. Something in his tone made her think that his memories were not all that matter-of-fact. Some hidden emotion flickered under the surface.

"Did you know Varina before Ben married her?" There was an intensity about her questioning that she couldn't control. The past had overtaken her in some weird fashion and made her a part of it. She had to search for answers that would bring the past and present together.

"Yeah, I knew her," Griff said gruffly. He looked around the kitchen as if noting changes that had been made.

"How long has it been since you were in this house?"

He shrugged. "I never came up much after the resort closed. Varina withdrew from everybody when she lost the money Ben left her. She was the one who had all her property tied up in the venture. The ski resort was her dream from the time she married Ben. After it went bankrupt, she kinda turned her back on everyone." Lynne thought she detected a softness in his eyes. "Wouldn't let anyone help her. A proud woman."

His eyes focused on some unseen point and then shifted back to Lynne. "I'd best be on my way."

"Won't you sit down and have a cup of coffee?"

He shook his bushy head and headed down the hall toward the front door without answering. What kind of a nerve had she touched, she asked herself as she watched him drive away in a battered Ford Cherokee.

She closed the door and walked slowly back to the kitchen. She would have something to share with Jarrett, she thought, happy to see that it was almost three o'clock. Hesitant to compete with his culinary talents, she decided to bake chicken breasts and make a casserole of potatoes au gratin. A can of pears would have to do for a salad, she decided. The kitchen echoed with homey clatter as she prepared the meal and set the oven timer to begin baking at five o'clock and shut off at six.

Surely he'd be back by then, she thought. She wandered into the library, tried to read but couldn't keep her mind on the book. The afternoon sun had vanished behind thickening clouds and without the bright sunshine the day had grown dreary.

At five o'clock she went upstairs and changed into a purple wool dress with a matching jacket. Chiding herself for the fluttering in her stomach, she took the time to sweep her hair up in a French roll and pin it in place with silver clips. How would he react after last night? Had he experienced the explosive desire, the same insatiable hunger? Was he as bewildered as she was by the unexplained attraction that had made them lovers? As she stared in the mirror, she remembered how she had seen and felt his touch, only to have it disappear when she turned around and held out her arms to open air. But last night was no illusion. The night of lovemaking belonged to the present. And no quirk of time was going to take it from her.

As she went downstairs, shadows like night creatures had crept into the hall and corners of the house. She heard needled branches scraping against the outside as the wind tossed them with increased violence. Buffeted by a bank of cold air sweeping down from the surrounding peaks, the house responded with moans and creaks of protest.

Lynne felt a chill coming out of the front room as she passed. She hurried into the library and coaxed a stubborn fire with tiny pieces of kindling until it was ready to take a cut log. Then she sat down on the leather couch and watched the yellow flames. What was it

Jarrett had said about watching a fire? *Expands an awareness of life's mysteries.*

She leaned her head back against the cushion. Tired from her afternoon's exertions, she closed her eyes. On the edge of sleep, her contentment faded. A terrifying sensation of being asleep and not able to wake up suddenly rendered her helpless. Like a jagged fork of lightning, danger assaulted her senses. Cries of panic crowded into her throat as someone viciously attacked her.

CHAPTER EIGHT

The assault came from all directions at once. Claw-like hands tore at her clothes and she could feel the cloth ripping away from her body. Sharp nails bit into her flesh leaving raw scratches across her breasts. She knew that she was screaming but no sounds came from her lips. A blow caught her on the side of her head, and she was unable to ward off the vicious attack. Her body disintegrated into floating pieces. Like someone struggling in slow motion, she writhed and twisted in an eternity of torment from which there was no escape. Fire exploded behind her eyes, and at that instant the mist suddenly parted. She saw the glint of a gun pointing down at her.

With a soundless scream, she bolted into a sitting position on the sofa. Her heart drummed wildly in her ears and clammy moisture beaded on her forehead. She sent a frantic glance around the empty room. With trembling hands she touched her purple dress. It was whole and undamaged. She felt the smooth French roll of her hair, still perfectly in place. Utterly bewildered, she looked at her arms, which smarted from deep scratches—only to see that her skin was smooth and unbroken. She was fully clothed and unharmed. She glanced at the clock. It was only ten minutes past five.

And yet it seemed as if an eternity had passed. Adrenaline still poured through her body and her breath was short. Already the frightening images were fading. But one thing remained—raw terror. An evil miasma permeated the room. The danger was no longer imagined.

"Leave!" The command came with the force of an electric shock.

She ran out of the room and up the stairs. She slammed the door to her bedroom and leaned up against it as if the mere weight of her body could keep out the unseen force that had assaulted her.

Later, she couldn't remember packing a bag or having any rational thoughts about where she was going. Hypnotized by fear, she was no longer in control of her own actions. She reached the front door, opened it and then looked back.

The little boy was standing in the hall. He still clutched the one-eared teddy bear and his face was puckered with sadness as he looked up at her. His wordless plea was unmistakable. "Don't go...stay."

Pain knotted her chest. Even though she couldn't rationalize her feelings, the phantom child had captured her on a level she didn't understand. She desperately wanted to bring laughter back into his face, protect him from the terror she had seen in his eyes. The appeal to give into the pleading in his eyes was strong, but she heard her strangled voice echoing in the empty house. "I can't...I can't."

She fled around the house to the garage, where she had put her car upon her return from Wolverton. Varina's cream-colored Subaru was parked on one side. Lynne remembered her saying that a friend had driven her to the Denver airport. The shadowy garage smelled of gas, oil, dirt and cobwebs.

She threw her suitcase into the back seat of her car and slid behind the steering wheel. She paused a moment to catch her breath. Jarrett? What about Jarrett? She put her hands to her temples and pressed against the swirling vertigo that was blotting out all reasoning. Before she could handle the onset of rational thought, she was violently jerked back in the seat.

When her eyes swam into focus, a mountain landscape was whizzing by the windows of the car. Suddenly she was in the back seat of a new-smelling Studebaker, sitting behind the young male driver and a pretty redhead in her twenties. He was hunched over the steering wheel and his head wobbled as if he were having trouble holding it erect. It was as if all strength had gone out of his body. An expression of horror twisted his face as the car careened out of control around the sharp curves of a mountain pass. Beside him the young woman screamed hysterically.

The car swerved from one side of the narrow road to the other on screeching tires. Every hairpin turn brought them closer and closer to the edge of a sheer cliff that dropped away to a canyon thousands of feet below. The fatal curve was too sharp, came too fast.

''We're going over,'' he cried in a slurred voice.

The feeble posts of a guardrail splintered and flew in the air. The car dropped over the precipice, tumbling over and over into the chasm thousands of feet below. A deafening crunch of metal accompanied a fiery explosion and a billow of black smoke rose from the wreckage.

Lynne screamed as she was jerked forward. Her ears rang with the sounds of grinding metal and shattering glass. Sobs burst from her throat, and her body shivered uncontrollably. She struggled to focus her eyes as her hands clutched the steering wheel. Slowly the windshield cleared as a gray mist thinned and then disappeared.

She looked about in bewilderment. She was in the shadowy garage, sitting in her own car and still holding the ignition key in her hand. The only sound was the strangled gasps of her own breathing. She let her head slump forward. It had happened again. She had been swept backward into another dimension of time and space. She cried out as the passenger door jerked open. Still caught in the throes of the frightening experience, she couldn't make her eyes focus.

"It's me." Jarrett reached for her. "Don't be frightened."

With a tremendous sob, she moved into the safe haven of his arms. He stroked her head, murmuring, "There now...take it easy." His fingers lightly threaded her hair as he held her close.

The textured weave of his jacket rubbed her cheek reassuringly, and the steady rise and fall of his chest validated the reality of his presence. She clung to him as an anchor, afraid to close her eyes, fearful that she would become disoriented again. He murmured reassurances, kissed her forehead and let his fingertips sensuously caress the curve of her neck. His warm breath touched her cheeks, bringing a tingling to her skin as the heat of his body eased away her chill. Like frost melting under a warm sun, the tremors of her body began to fade.

"Better now?"

She nodded, still clinging to his firm solid body.

"Now, tell me what happened," he ordered rather sternly, as if he were prepared to deal harshly with anyone guilty of sending her into such a fright. "I heard you screaming when I drove up."

Lynne's thoughts were sluggish as she sought to explain an experience that was beyond the realm of belief.

Jarrett grew impatient with her silence. "Why were you sitting in your car screaming?" He glanced at the suitcase in the back seat. "Were you leaving?"

Her reply was barely audible. "Yes."

"Why?"

She frowned. Something had happened in the house...in the library. A nightmare. A personal threat of some kind. The terrifying emotions remained. Images hovered on the edge of her consciousness like a bad dream lost in the mist of sleep, so faint she couldn't verbalize them. She pressed her fingers against her forehead and tried to bring them back into focus. Nothing. Only a residue of fear.

"Why were you leaving?" Jarrett repeated.

"I...I don't know," she answered honestly. "There was danger."

"A noise?" he prodded.

He wanted a simple explanation and she couldn't give him one. She remembered fleeing to her bedroom, coming down the stairs, and then—the little boy was there! That part she remembered clearly. He had begged her to stay. Even now she felt the pull of his pitiful plea, *Please stay.* But she had refused, turned her back on him and hurried out to the garage.

And before she could drive away, two young people riding to their death had claimed her.

She must have stiffened, for he said, "It's all right. Just tell me what happened." He put his hands on her shoulders and turned her toward him.

She frowned. A young man...a pretty redheaded woman. Lynne's eyes rounded. That's how Griff had described Benny's mother—"pretty redhead." Lynne gasped. "Benny's parents. Dave and Carole Mitchell. That's who they were."

Jarrett's hands tightened on her shoulders. "What are you talking about?"

She searched his face. Was that anger or concern that flickered in his cheek muscles? She sensed a resentment in him. As if he thought she were trying to manipulate him. Did she dare try to explain? She moistened her lips. "A young couple driving down a mountain road were killed when the brakes failed. The car went off the cliff...and exploded. I think...I think they were Benny Mitchell's parents."

Jarrett's jaw worked as if he were trying to keep his voice even. "That must have been nearly thirty years ago. Why are you all stirred up about something that happened around the time you were born?"

Her courage failed her. *Because it's happening to me, now!* she cried silently. How could she make him understand that she had been in that car? She took a deep breath and looked straight into the shadowed depths of his eyes.

"I . . . I was in the car with them."

He looked darkly perplexed. "Why would you imagine such a thing?"

"I didn't imagine it!" she flared. "I mean . . . I didn't create it in my own mind. It happened—" She broke off in frustration. She knew it didn't make sense. Nobody in her right mind . . . *in her right mind*. Suddenly she was too tired to wrestle with the logical explanations. The images were almost gone now, like negatives turned dark and unreadable. She was glad that the living nightmare would soon be lost in her subconscious. Jarrett had every right to be skeptical.

"You've let this house get the better of you. Reading all those old newspapers has gotten you all worked up—fired your imagination. The people who lived in this house—Benjamin, his son and daughter-in-law, his grandson, Benny—they're all *dead.*" His voice landed firmly on the word *dead.* "Why have you let the house get such a hold on you?"

She searched his face. Why did she sense that he was trying to slay a demon of his own? His guarded eyes told her that he was not nearly as detached from the situation as he pretended. And why did her mind carry a memory of him that was too strong to deny? Even though she had slept in his arms, given herself to him as she had no other man, he still remained a stranger. Prickling with cold, unreasonable suspicion, she wondered if he was somehow responsible for a mental and emotional manipulation that dominated her senses.

Unconsciously, she drew back from his touch.

"Now you're looking at me as if somehow I'll sprout horns and a forked tail at any moment," he said in an accusing tone.

"You don't understand—"

"How can I," he demanded, "when you refuse to give me a reasonable explanation?"

Reasonable? Yes, of course. How simple it sounded. That's all he wanted. A logical, rational explanation would satisfy him—only she didn't have one. She took a deep breath. Her emotions were back under control. She would give him what he wanted. "You're right, I'm being overly sensitive. Melodramatic. I confess to letting my imagination run away with me."

"You don't seem like the type to me," he said bluntly. "I'll admit there's a fascination about the house but I don't see anything to cause such flights of fear. I'm beginning to think you've convinced yourself that the house is haunted."

"As you pointed out so emphatically, all four Mitchells and the Ashley girls are dead." It was no use adding, *You don't see them, but I do.*

She opened the car door on her side. "Let's go in the house. I have dinner ready." She strode ahead. Her stomach tightened as she entered the front hall. Vibrations echoed in her mind, seeming to come from the very walls themselves. Was that mocking laughter? The house would not release her. Something outside of time itself held her there. Something clouded deeply in the past swirled around her and she was helpless to deny the house its revenge.

"I'll take your bag back upstairs," he said, coming up behind her, using a rather stiff tone as if he weren't certain how to relate to her anymore.

The afternoon's seesaw of emotions had left her empty. When she entered the kitchen and saw the little boy standing by the window, smiling at her, she didn't even flinch with surprise.

The glow on his face reached out to take her like a splash of sunlight. *You came back.* With a feeling of detachment, she knew that there was no escape as long as he needed her. She had tried to leave him but had been defeated. The realization brought a strange kind of relief, as if she'd been wrong to try to run away. Some force beyond understanding had stopped her—and brought her back. With a resigned sigh, she accepted the truth that the house had a hold on her she couldn't break. She gave him a surrendering smile. *You win.*

"What are you doing looking out the window with a wistful smile on your face?" asked Jarrett, walking up behind her. He looked over her shoulder. "Oh, I see . . . beautiful sunset, isn't it?"

A bright crimson glow bathed the mountain peaks. The afternoon storm had passed. Clouds like pink whales floated across the horizon and the sky held a luminous sheen like a rich silk print. For a long moment they stood there in peaceful contentment, looking out the kitchen window—*just the way they'd enjoyed the spectacular day's end many times!*

Her patience snapped. She swung around and faced him. *Who are you?* Just like the little boy and his grandfather, this stranger—this lover—had been manipulating her from the moment she saw him standing in the doorway with skis on his shoulders. But he was no phantom. The breathless ecstasy, the spiraling passion she'd felt in his arms as they made love had been real. His existence was in the flesh, but the memories she held of him belonged to another time. With sickening certainty she knew that he was a part of the bewildering company of ghosts parading in and out of her consciousness. Her eyes snapped with unspoken accusations as she stared at him.

"Lynne?" His voice was a soft caress. He started to slip his arms around her.

"Don't touch me."

Slowly he dropped his arms.

"Who are you?" Her voice was harsh. She could not have imagined the intensity behind his casual, charming manner. Something deeper lay hidden just below the surface.

He cocked his head slightly to one side. "What kind of a question is that? You know damn well who I am. Is this some kind of game—twenty questions?"

"I have only one question—why did you come here, pretending to be a stranger to the house?"

"Pretending?" His dark eyebrows rose. "What in the hell are you talking about?"

"I'm talking about the way you knew your way around that first day. About your trips to the attic. I'm talking about—" Her voice was rising. She swallowed to bring it under control. "I don't know how to explain it, but—"

"But what?" His reasonable tone mocked her. How could she tell him about the scenes that flitted through her mind as memories. *I've known you before.* The words caught in her throat and wouldn't come out.

He reached out and pulled her close. "Relax... relax," he ordered as she pushed against his chest. He held her firmly against him and she was no match for his physical strength. For the first time she realized how precarious her situation had become. She forced herself to quit struggling. As she went limp, he said in a quiet tone, "That's better. Now look at me!"

Slowly she raised her eyes to his.

"Before three days ago, I had never been in this house." His look was clear and guileless. He didn't blink and neither did she. She stared at his handsome face, his wonderfully dark eyes and warm mobile lips. How did she know he was lying?

"You don't believe me?"

"Of course I do," she said too quickly. She stepped back and this time he let her go. "I'm sorry. I guess my imagination is working overtime."

"You really ought to find out what's causing those nightmares," he said gently.

She gave him a measured smile. "That's exactly what I intend to do." She turned away and walked across the kitchen, her back straight and a determined thrust to her chin. "I smell the chicken. I hope you're hungry."

"Famished."

"Good." She tried to put some enthusiasm into setting the kitchen table and serving the meal she had prepared earlier in the day, but the joy was gone. The atmosphere was strained. He attempted to keep the conversation going but her thoughts were like pretzels, twisting and turning in every direction.

"Griff was here today," she said abruptly.

"Who?"

"Hugh Griffin, the *Wolverton Weekly* editor."

"Oh, yeah. The guy who gave you the papers. Where are they, by the way? I'd like to have a look at them."

"Why?"

He raised an eyebrow. "Why not? You found them interesting, maybe I will, too. For heaven's sake, why are you so damn prickly? What have I done to deserve such dagger looks?"

"I just have the feeling that your interest in the Mitchell family isn't strictly business."

He started to say something and then thought better of it. "What did this Griffin guy want?"

Knowing he was evading her question, she sighed and said, "I'm not sure. I was out for a walk and was looking over the old buildings when he showed up. Somehow I got the impression that he didn't expect to be caught snooping around. I thought I saw someone in the old lodge before the roof fell in."

"You didn't go in any of those old buildings— they're death traps!"

"Of course I didn't." His commanding tone irked her. "I'm just telling you that I was as surprised to see Griff as he was to see me. He said that he was just refreshing his memory."

"Probably getting some ideas for an article," finished Jarrett. "Since the word is out that some new investors may be found, I wouldn't be surprised if he's working on a half-truth, half-rumor news story. It's a wonder that he hasn't tried to catch me for an interview. It's no secret I'm staying here."

"He didn't ask where you were." She eyed him with a measuring frankness. "I don't think you've ever told me how you got this assignment. You said you'd never been in this part of Colorado."

"True. But I spend a couple of skiing vacations in southern Colorado every year... Purgatory Ski Resort. There's a name for you. Anyway, I met some investors looking over an area on nearby Wolf Creek Pass. They showed me an old brochure of the defunct Conifer Ridge Ski Resort. Asked me if I wanted to check it out—and here I am."

There was more to the story. He was leaving out something. She searched the hidden depths of his eyes.

"Delicious chicken," he murmured, challenging her skeptical look. "And what else did our small-town editor have to say?"

"You've met him before, haven't you?"

He laid down his fork in exasperation. "What is it with you? No, I've never met the man. Did he say that I had?"

"No. Your name never came up," she admitted. "But when he came in the house, he acted a lot like you did the first time."

"And how was that?"

"Like...like you were refreshing your memory. The room that's locked—you said it was probably a den or game room."

"So?"

"You were right. Griff knew where the key was." Jarrett raised a questioning eyebrow.

"Above the door. Anyway, there's a gun rack in the room. That's probably why Varina locked it up. Griff admitted that he used to be a frequent visitor before the resort went bankrupt. I had the impression he might have been sweet on Varina. She was a young widow about his own age at that time. They could have been sweethearts."

He gave her an amused smile. "I think you're an incurable romantic." He reached out and covered her hand. "And more sensitive to other people than is good for you."

She stiffened and withdrew her hand. "You think I'm nuts. Admit it. Not that I blame you. You come back, find me shivering in my car, blabbing about two people who died in a car crash nearly thirty years ago. And I'll tell you something else, too." Words tumbled out of her mouth like a runaway express train. "I was driven out of the house! Driven! Something... something evil attacked me."

"Take it easy," he soothed. "Where did this happen?"

"In the library."

He was out of his chair and round the table before she took her next breath. "Come on." He pulled her to her feet. "Let's face this dragon...now." With a firm arm around her waist, he propelled her down the hall.

She hung back when they reached the library doorway.

"It's all right," he said. "I want to show you that there's absolutely nothing in this room...or this house...to frighten you."

She looked around the darkly paneled library. *Nothing now.* Nothing to cause the bone-shaking chill that was creeping into her limbs. In the fireplace, glowing red embers radiated heat into the room. On the wall, the old clock ticked away in a comforting rhythm.

"Sit down." Jarrett eased her onto the couch, and his arms surrounded her in a protective embrace. She felt his warm breath on her face, and the faint odor of a spicy cologne touched her nostrils with familiar reassurance. "Now tell me what happened."

She worked her lower lip. "I was waiting for time to pass...waiting for you to come. And I was sitting here, thinking about last night."

He nodded and waited.

"And then..." Her mouth went dry as her body remembered. Deep within her subconscious, cues triggered a quickening pulse and her palms grew moist. All of the blurred images and terror existed out of any perception of time. Like alien forces they collided in her mind with a shattering impact.

He tightened his arms as he felt her tremble. "Tell me," he whispered. "What's happening?"

She tried to draw forth some concrete basis for the malevolent, hate-filled residue of her terror, but couldn't. "I heard myself screaming. I remember touching my clothes and my hair... as if I expected them to be torn off. I was out of my mind with terror. I don't remember packing a suitcase, but I must have."

"Sleepwalking," he said in a matter-of-fact tone. "That has to be it. You fell asleep here on the couch. And while you were sleeping you had a nightmare." He smoothed her hair back from her moist forehead. "Don't you see what happened, sweetheart? Caught up in the midst of a frightening dream, you packed your suitcase, went out to your car. Still asleep, you sat there and continued the dream—until I came and woke you up." He let his fingers stroke her cheek. "This sleep-walking tendency is a symptom of stress. There's nothing in the house to harm you."

Suddenly she was too tired, too spent of emotion to argue. He gently pressed her head against his shoulder and wrapped his arms around her. Slowly the warmth of his body invaded hers, and with it came peace. Peace from all the emotional upheaval. Blessed release from the insidious presentiment of danger. As he bent and kissed her forehead, all doubts and suspicions faded. With relief, she slipped her arms around his neck. It didn't matter whether he belonged to the past, present or future. Real or phantom, she no longer cared. She closed her eyes as he picked her up and carried her back to the tiny, messy bedroom.

CHAPTER NINE

She came awake slowly the next morning, pleasantly aware of the man lying beside her. A smile curved her lips as she hugged the warmth of his sleeping body. All the barriers, all the protection, all the caution that had guarded her from such complete physical and emotional surrender to any lover had been leveled. Her defenses were no longer in place. Never in her life had she felt so complete...yet so vulnerable. She knew nothing about the depths of Jarrett's feelings for her. He kept his own counsel and she knew little more about him than she had on their first meeting. Except on an intimate level, he remained a stranger, acting very much like a man with a guarded secret. Even in moments of intimate sharing, she had sensed a withholding, as if he dared not reveal himself completely. Nothing in the situation promised anything but a fragile happiness that could be wrestled from her at any moment.

As she stirred in the three-quarter bed, she unwittingly jabbed an elbow into Jarrett's chest. One of his deep blue eyes came open with a twinkling glint as he faced her on the pillow. "Do you always hog the bed?"

"Look who's talking?" she chided. His warm body had hers pinned against the wall. He flung one arm across her chest and one leg across her hips. She moved her face closer to his. "Not that I'm complaining." She smiled, her lips full and gently bruised.

He groaned. "Lady, stop looking at me like that."

"Like what?" she murmured innocently, snuggling in closer, her breasts rounded against the soft tufts of black hair on his chest. The sensation of being in his arms in the morning was familiar. Her body remembered the wonderful closeness starting each day even if her mind did not.

His hands slid around her and he trailed his fingers over her slender back, tracing the soft curves of her waist and thighs. "Perfect," he murmured, tasting the soft lobe of her ear. His mouth found hers and her breath was cut off in a long and lingering kiss. Yes, he was the lover that her body had welcomed—now and always. Wrapped in his embrace, she accepted the wondrous knowledge that in some undefined way he had always belonged to her. Morning love was the best, she thought as they melted together in a celebration of a new and wonderful day.

A short while later, he reluctantly slipped out of bed and dressed while she lay there dozing, warm and content. She hadn't stirred by the time he came back with a cup of coffee. "Wake up, you slothful woman. If you're not out of the bed in ten minutes—"

"Yes?" Her luminous eyes challenged him.

He leaned over and tweaked her nose affectionately. "I'll climb back in bed with you."

"Promises, promises."

He laughed, picked up her clothes, hastily thrown in a heap the night before and tossed them to her.

"How about loaning me a robe to put on?"

He eyed her bare shoulders mischievously. "What if I said no? Would you treat me to the sight of a naked nymph running up the stairs? I'd love to see Duchamp's painting in the flesh."

She stared at him, her mouth suddenly dry. *We viewed* Nude Descending a Staircase *together.* She even remembered that she'd bought a white linen dress for their trip to Philadelphia. They had stayed at a lovely hotel within walking distances of all the historical landmarks. And before going sightseeing at the art gallery, they'd made love in the hotel room—just like this morning.

She looked up at him, swallowing against a choking feeling in her throat. "Have you seen the original of that painting?"

"No. Only reprints. Why?"

She forced a casual shrug. She was afraid to tell him about the aberrations of her mind. She couldn't accuse him of not remembering something that had never happened.

"Why the frown?" He bent over and kissed her lightly. "I like it better when you're not as solemn as a judge. Breakfast in fifteen minutes." He tossed her a robe.

She put it on and walked slowly upstairs. All feelings of warm contentment were gone. She feared that the nights in Jarrett's arms might be only a fantasy like the one of visiting the art gallery together. Would she awaken one of these mornings and find that everything that had happened between her and Jarrett was just another memory, one without any reality? What had happened to her that she couldn't distinguish between actual experiences and memories that were as real as the rhythm of her heartbeat?

As she showered and dressed, her mind whirled. How could the past, present and events that had never happened be contained within the walls of this dark house? She stood in front of the mirror, tying a pretty yellow scarf over the shoulders of her knit sweater, when she realized that the decor of the room had changed. The wallpaper was now the pretty lavender spriggy pattern, and frilly Priscilla curtains swept across the window. So smooth was the transition this time that her heart didn't miss a beat. There was no fog. Just the reflection of the little boy standing behind her.

Benny's wide eyes popped with merriment as he fixed his gaze on some point beyond her. He gave a childish wave and then covered his mouth as if to hide a giggle. He bounded forward, and on the edge of Lynne's peripheral vision she saw a pair of arms sweep him up. A flash of red hair, a blur of shadows and a second later nothing remained in the mirror except her own reflection and the room with its ugly floral wallpaper and heavy drapes.

Lynne sat on the edge of her bed, strangely calm. For a few brief seconds, she had slipped backward in time again. She had been a part of something that had happened in this room when Benny and his mother were alive. She had shared in the love between them in the same way she had shared in the little boy's terror at another time. In some bewildering way, time was out of sync. She knew with sickening certainty that Jarrett was a part of that same time warp. She didn't understand any of it.

He was on the telephone as she went downstairs and passed the library on her way to the kitchen. She heard him spouting off figures with the rapidity of a talking calculator. His tone was brisk, curt and aggressive—a sharp contrast to the lover murmuring softly in her ear.

In the kitchen, hot cereal, toast and Canadian bacon waited on the stove. She saw he had cleaned up last night's dishes. In a few minutes he joined her at the table, but he ate quickly with an air of distraction. She could tell that his mind was elsewhere. He excused himself with a brief kiss to her hairline and went back to the library.

Despite a passionate night of love, he seemed to be a stranger again. How could she know him so intimately, and yet not know him at all? Her attempts to learn about his personal life had only brought vague answers or light quips that told her nothing.

When she brought him a cup of hot coffee a few minutes later, he mumbled a vague "thank you." He was studying some maps spread out on the library table. His eyebrows were pulled together in a tight frown. She could feel tension radiating from him.

She stifled the impulse to ask him what was the matter. His profile was one of granite lines and planes. She didn't know how to respond to the distance suddenly stretching between them. He created too many emotions in her. She felt pulled in conflicting directions. He was her lover—and a stranger.

He gave her an impatient smile as she stood staring at him. "What is it?" His voice was strained.

"Nothing," she lied, and left the room.

Later today she would talk to him. What was causing her sense of uneasiness? The conviction that he wasn't being honest with her? That in some way he was manipulating her now...and from some point in her past? Ridiculous, she told herself, but the conviction lingered.

The telephone rang several times as she worked in the kitchen and she wondered how close he was to finishing his report. Another day or two—perhaps. If the project went through, he might be back from time to time, she reasoned, refusing to give in to the sense of loss already stabbing at her. But what if the investors turned thumbs-down. Would it all be over? Would he pack up and leave? And would the house let her go? Or was she trapped in a dimension of time from which there was no escape?

She heard the telephone ring again and was surprised when he came into the kitchen.

"Call for you, Lynne. Somebody with a Southern drawl as thick as chicken gumbo."

Lynne gave a delighted laugh. "Dixie." She threw down her dish towel.

"A friend, I take it?"

"The best." She started for the phone.

"I need to check the lift...be back in a few minutes," he told her as she bounded into the library.

"Hi, Dixie, what a nice surprise," Lynne said with a happy laugh in her voice.

"Heavens to betsy, you don't sound like the same gal I talked to a couple days back." Dixie's tone was almost accusing, as if she'd been the butt of some joke. "Here I was thinking you might be needing a bit of cheering up, being in that house all *alone* and all."

There was a puzzled frankness in her voice that made Lynne swallow back a chuckle. She knew Dixie was dying to know who had answered the phone.

"I'm glad you called." Lynne smiled to herself, wondering just how long it would be before her friend's curiosity got the best of her and Dixie asked her right out, "Who is that man?" Lynne could picture her round face creased in curiosity.

"I thought I must have the wrong number," Dixie said. "I called several times and the phone was busy."

"Oh, Jarrett was making a few business calls."

"Jarrett?"

Lynne grinned. Even over the phone, Dixie's avid interest sparked like Forth of July fireworks. "Yes, Jarrett Taylor."

"And if you don't mind me asking, who in tarnation is Jarrett Taylor?"

Lynne decided she'd teased her enough. "An investment analyst. Very charming. Very handsome. And *my* houseguest."

"Houseguest?" Dixie echoed in utter disbelief. "You let some good-looking fellow move in with you? Am I speaking to Lynne Delevan, the gal who puts up pointed stakes around herself and is ready to pour boiling oil on any male trying to scale her walls?"

Lynne laughed. "The same."

"All right, fill me in," she ordered. "From the suppressed excitement in your voice, he's a kin to Mark Harmon or Tom Cruise."

"Even better. He's…he's everything I ever thought a man should be." Her voice quivered. "I love him, Dixie."

"Easy, gal. Some guy shows up when you're stuck in a house way out in God knows where. You put out the welcome mat and suddenly your head's in a tailspin. Sounds to me like you're setting yourself up for a crash landing."

"I don't think so," Lynne said with as much conviction as she could manage.

"Honey, I know you. You're not cut out for that 'my place or yours' casual stuff. Especially with someone you hardly know."

"I've known him before."

"You have?" Her voice registered surprise. "I don't remember your mentioning anyone by that name. Where'd you meet?"

"I didn't mean I'd actually met him." Lynne's voice trailed off. Dixie would never understand the flashes of intuitive memory that surrounded this stranger. "He's the kind of guy you fantasize about," she finished up lamely.

"What's he doing in a place like Wolverton?" she asked, openly skeptical.

"I told you about the defunct ski resort. Well, Jarrett's looking it over for some investors. They may put it back in operation." She let her glance travel over the mess of papers, maps and drawings. "He's using the library for an office."

"What about that Mitchell gal? Does she know about this . . . guest?"

"Of course. No problem. I called her before I let him have a room. She was glad to know there was a possibility that the resort might get some new financing. I think she lost a bundle when the place went bankrupt. Anyway, she said it was okay. It's been wonderful to have Jarrett in the house."

"I admit you sound a hundred percent better than the last time I called. I thought that place really had you spooked. Sounded to me as if you expected to see ghosts and all that other haunting stuff found in old houses."

If you only knew. For a moment, Lynne couldn't say anything.

In the silence, Dixie sighed. "Well, gal, I guess I can stop worrying about you." A trace of uneasiness still remained in her tone but she brightened. "Let me know how things go."

"Quit worrying, will you? Aren't you the one who's been preaching at me to loosen up and put a little excitement in my life?"

"Yes, but—" She broke off. "Okay, honey, go for it. But remember, vacation romances don't wear well . . . or long."

They chatted for a few minutes about office gossip and Lynne was smiling when she hung up. She put the phone back on the desk, and as she turned around, she glanced at the library table where Jarrett had spread out some large maps. One was a colorful relief map where someone had drawn in ski trails and named them. Devil's Run. Pebble Run. Buttermilk.

Buttermilk.

A jolt went through her. She stared at the map. That was the ski trail her memory had delivered the first day when she'd been caught up in the memory of skiing down the mountainside outside the kitchen window... before she even knew there was such a run named Buttermilk. Where had the knowledge come from?

Caught in a mesmerizing mental whirlpool, she was filled with an urgency that made her hurry down the hall and out the front door. She had to ask Jarrett about the name.

There was little warmth coming from the morning sun and she hugged herself against a gust of cold air sweeping down into the valley. She should go back and get a wrap, she thought as she walked down the front steps, propelled by a tension that was producing its own heat.

She saw him standing by the old lift at the base of the nearby slope. Bounding quickly down the rest of the front steps, she ran toward him. "Jarrett," she called and waved to him. Her breath came in short gasps as she ran at full speed toward him.

"Whoa. Whoa. Where's the fire?" His tone was light but his eyes were anxious as his arms went around her shoulder and he looked down into her flushed face.

"I ... I had to talk ... to you."

"I've been gone all of fifteen minutes," he teased. "You're shivering. Why on earth didn't you put on a coat? Here." He slipped out of his jacket and put it over her shoulders. "Your teeth are beginning to chatter." He kept an arm around her shoulder as they began walking back toward the house. "Now what do you want to talk about?"

"That map ... on the table. With the names of the ski runs."

"Yes, what about it?"

"The names given to the old trails—I mean, did the defunct ski resort have a run named Buttermilk ... like the one marked on the map?"

He looked puzzled by the intensity of her expression. "No. I was identifying some possible new runs. Just threw in some names for identification instead of calling them trail one, trail two, and so on. What's the matter, sweetheart, do you have something against Buttermilk?"

"How could I have known that one of them was called Buttermilk before I looked at the map?"

"Well, it's not a unique name. Either Vail or Aspen has a Buttermilk mountain, I think. You probably heard the name and it stuck in your memory."

Memory. He tightened his arm around her as she shivered and said, "I remember skiing down a run named Buttermilk."

"You do? In Aspen or Vail?"

"No...it was right over there." She stopped and pointed to the wooden hillside where Buttermilk had been marked on the map.

His mouth tightened as he followed her pointing finger. No trail scarred that particular slope—because it hadn't been built yet.

"That's impossible," he said.

"I know," she said quietly. "I don't even ski."

They walked back to the house in silence.

Lunch was a quiet affair. Jarrett kept sending furtive glances at her, and she felt an unnamed weight resting on her shoulders. She had tried to shrug it off— and had failed. Even though it was impossible, her memory was *not* faulty. The sensation of skiing down that mountain was as clear as anything she had ever experienced.

She avoided his eyes as she listlessly bit into her tuna sandwich. *He thinks I'm nuts.* She sighed heavily. *Maybe I am. Is this how insanity begins?*

He set down his coffee cup. "Don't get yourself worked up over nothing. The mind is a tricky thing. I'm sure there's a logical explanation. You'll have a good laugh when you figure it out."

"I could use one about now," she admitted with a wry smile.

He picked up his plate, walked over to the sink and rinsed it. He seemed to be avoiding looking at her. She had a sick feeling in the pit of her stomach. *I'm not crazy...I'm not.*

"Guess I'd better get back to work. I need to finalize my report."

Finalize? That meant he'd be leaving soon. She nodded.

He stopped by her chair and put his hands lightly on her shoulders. "Why don't you catch up on your sleep this afternoon?"

Sleep? She suppressed a tremor. *And perchance to dream? Aye, there's the rub.* She'd never really understood Hamlet's dread before—now it had become her own. What if she had another sleepwalking trauma? Jarrett was already uneasy about her bizarre behavior. She couldn't chance another episode like yesterday's.

She forced a light laugh. "I'll admit sleep was on the short side last night, but I think some housecleaning is in order. You get back to your report and I'll deal with a mop and broom."

He pulled her to her feet and kissed her. His lips teased hers with hungry intent and they were both breathing heavily when he slowly lifted his mouth from hers. "That's a down payment." He ran a light finger down the slope of her nose. "See you later."

The warmth of his kiss stayed with her as she tackled the kitchen chores. She even scrubbed the oven where her scalloped potatoes had run over the afternoon before. The meal had been less than a success but the evening had ended in perfect joy. Several times she heard the phone ring and heard Jarrett's muffled voice floating down the hall. She pushed aside a threatening loneliness. Time enough to face the empty days and nights after he left.

She stripped the narrow bed of its sheets and made it up fresh. She wondered if they would share the same bed tonight.

She gathered up his dirty clothes for a second load of laundry, dusted off the chest of drawers and night table and swept the wide-planked floor. As she ran the broom under the bed, she realized that something had been shoved under it. Getting down on her knees, she glimpsed a dusty box, the kind that might have held a pair of boots. The lid was dusty but showed signs of recent handprints as she pulled out the box and opened it.

Photographs. Nearly a hundred of them stuffed into the old box. For a long minute she just sat there on the floor staring at the photos. The one on top showed a group of laughing people standing on the steps of the house. A tall man with his arm around a pretty dark-haired woman was recognizable—Benjamin Mitchell. A young man with craggy features who sat on the bottom step surely must have been a young Griff without a beard but she couldn't be sure.

She thumbed through a few more without being able to identify the scenery or the people. Thoughtfully, she closed the lid of the box and just sat there. Why was the box of old pictures hidden under Jarrett's bed? A tight feeling quivered under her breastbone.

She got to her feet, walked to the kitchen and dumped the photos on the table. Sitting down, she started sorting them into piles, and the history of the Mitchell family began to emerge. She suspected that many of the photographs were taken in Texas when

Benjamin had been married to his first wife. The Colorado scenes were easy to identify because of the nearby jagged Sawtooth Mountains and the Victorian house in the background. There was even one of the new garage going up next to the house.

Lynne's hands trembled when she picked up a picture of a smiling couple holding a tiny baby. Even though it wasn't in color, she had no trouble recognizing the pretty young mother and Ben's tall son. She stared at the photograph and knew that her feelings about it were founded in something deep and personal. Her reaction to seeing the young couple with their new baby was strong, though the reason for a sudden rise of emotion was vague. It had something to do with yesterday's nightmare—this young couple, Dave and Carole Mitchell, had been a part of it. No images remained, yet Lynne's eyes filled with tears as she looked at the young man and woman smiling proudly as they showed off their tiny infant.

There were a few pictures of Benjamin holding his grandson on his lap and the toddler grinned into the camera. A wisp of a cowlick stood up at the back of the boy's dark head. The photograph didn't do justice to Benny's sparkling eyes and infectious smile, Lynne thought in a detached acceptance of her extrasensory knowledge of the child. There were several pictures of the little boy holding his teddy bear; none of the photos explained the terror she'd seen in his eyes as he clutched the one-eared stuffed toy.

There was a wedding picture of Benjamin and Varina in the parlor, standing in front of the fireplace, which was bedecked with flowers. A small, attractive young woman somewhere in her late twenties, Varina stood proudly beside the older man nearly twice her age. She wore a simple street-length dress with a wreath of flowers around her head. Another picture showed the wedding guests around the dining room table as the newlyweds cut a modest wedding cake. There was no mistaking the lanky editor this time. Griff's angular face was turned toward Varina and his expression made Lynne wonder about his feelings.

There were quite a number of pictures showing a ribbon cutting beneath the sign Welcome To Conifer Ridge Ski Resort. The scene was a startling contrast to the present ghost town buildings. Varina was the only person Lynne recognized in any of the photos. There was one of the lodge, festive with hanging flags and grinning skiers standing on the steps. The nearby shop windows were filled with merchandise and proud owners stood in the doorways, smiling broadly at the camera.

Lynne, lost in a reverie of the past, didn't hear Jarrett come into the kitchen.

"What are you doing with those pictures?" His tone was abrupt and accusing.

She met his gaze with a flash of anger that was as sharp as summer lightning. "No, the question is—what were *you* doing with them?"

CHAPTER TEN

Something dark clouded his blue eyes and then disappeared. "I was looking at them...what else? What's the problem?" He sat down beside her and gave her his disarming smile. "Does that condemning glare of yours mean that I've overstepped myself by showing interest in some old photos?"

"Where did you find them?"

"In one of the desk drawers. I was looking for a ruler and I—" He broke off with a short laugh. "Really, Lynne darling. What's the big deal? So I found a box of old photographs. Come on, lighten up. I haven't even had time to go through them. It isn't as if I were making off with the family silver, for heaven's sake."

His airy dismissal made her suspicions seem melodramatic. Yet there was a subtle edge to his voice that denied the teasing lilt of his explanation.

"What were the photographs doing under your bed?"

"If you must know, I was hiding them from *you*."

"Me?"

"Yes, you. To put it bluntly, Lynne, I'm concerned about the weird fixation you seem to have on this house and the Mitchell family." He leaned toward her.

"Please understand. I was only doing what I thought best."

Fixation? Is that what it was? He'd never believe that she had been drawn through some kind of a time tunnel to experience the past with the Mitchells. He was right about one thing; she had a compulsive need to find out everything she could about the house and the family.

In a firm tone, she dismissed his rationalizing. "I don't appreciate your hiding things from me."

"I was afraid that a bunch of old photographs might bring about more of those wild nightmares you've been having. So I stuck the box under my bed, thinking that the temptation to pore over the photos would be out of your way."

In spite of herself, she felt foolish at his frank admission. There was no sinister intent on his part; he was only trying to protect her. "I'm sorry. I guess I jumped to the wrong conclusion," she said, silently admitting that she must be getting paranoid.

He gave a wry smile as he surveyed her organized piles. "Is there some rhyme or reason to this project?"

"I'm sorting the pictures into a time line. I think some were taken while Benjamin lived in Texas with his first wife." She touched another pile. "These are Colorado scenes. See the house? Benjamin and his son are putting on the garage. Here's one taken of the proud parents, Dave and Carole, after the baby was born."

Jarrett looked at each one as she handed it to him. His expression remained bland but Lynne sensed that his attitude was a little bit too casual. The way the veins in his hands stood out as he held the photos indicated that he was more interested in them than he was willing to show her.

"After Benny's parents were killed, Benjamin married Varina. Here's a picture of their wedding. I think this fellow is Griffin...without his beard. Don't you think he's looking at Varina in a rather...lustful way?"

Jarrett laughed. "I'd be more inclined to think he'd had too much champagne." When Lynne didn't smile, he raised an eyebrow. "What are you suggesting—that Griffin had romantic feelings for Varina when she married Benjamin?"

"Maybe."

"The woman's been a widow for over twenty years. The man's had plenty of time to satisfy his yearnings."

"Maybe the feelings only went one way. Or maybe Varina took him as a lover instead of a husband." She ignored Jarrett's amused chuckle. "Here are several pictures of little Benny holding his teddy bear." Her voice was suddenly strained as an unexpected emotion overtook her. *That's just the way Benny looks when he's smiling.*

"What are you looking at so intently?" Jarrett asked, taking the pictures of Benny from her. He frowned as he studied them. "I don't see anything to account for that sudden anguish in your eyes."

She didn't try to explain. "Here's a photograph of Varina standing between the two sisters who were killed, Maribelle and Sue Ann Ashley."

"How do you know that's who they are?"

I've seen them! Very clearly she pictured them sitting on the green sofa, laughing and chatting, their long straight hair flowing down their backs, and their dresses falling to their ankles. She was positive they were wearing the same outfits in the picture.

"How do you know?" Jarrett repeated slowly.

"They look like sisters," she answered, avoiding his eyes. "This last pile shows the ski resort in operation." Lynne handed the photos to him. "Hard to believe the only thing that's left is some tumbledown buildings."

He glanced through them. "Too bad the venture went sour—the resort had the potential to be as successful as any other in Colorado."

"Is that what you're going to recommend to your client?"

"I have to get some more data before I decide." He handed back the pictures. "Any more?" he asked.

"No, the time line ends there. Either Varina stopped taking pictures after the bankruptcy or they're in another box." She began gathering them up.

"I wouldn't mind talking to this Griffin fellow. He might give me some good background information. Sometimes empirical data doesn't tell the whole story. What do you say we take a drive to the bustling town of Wolverton?" He touched a lock of hair that had drifted forward on her cheek. "I might even be persuaded to buy you a drink."

"At Nellie's Place?"

"Why not?"

"Why not," Lynne echoed. "I'll get my coat." She decided it would be interesting to see what happened when she walked into that bar with Jarrett at her side. Would he encounter the same antagonism the townspeople had shown her or would good old Nellie split a seam in her tight skirt just getting over to their table fast enough?

As they drove down the twisting road, Jarrett handled his rented Volvo with the ease of someone who enjoyed mountain driving. When Lynne commented about his relaxed skill, he talked about the northern mountains of New Mexico. "The state's not all sand and desert. You really should visit Taos and see the wonderful old Indian pueblo there."

"I'd love to."

His eyes met hers. "There's a lot of things I'd like to show you."

"Like the plaza in front of the Palace of the Governors?"

He shot her a startled look. "I thought you'd never been to Santa Fe?"

"I...I haven't. I must have read about it," she lied, trying to deny the memory of them walking hand in hand around the plaza. She wanted to say, *Don't you remember buying me a lovely squash-blossom necklace from one of the Indian vendors?* Instead she bit her lower lip and turned her face toward her window. Was she fantasizing—or remembering?

She forced herself back to the present. A moment later she gasped. "Stop. This is it."

He slowed. "What?"

She closed her eyes. *That is the curve! The place where she'd gone over the side of the cliff with Benny's parents.* The nightmare came lurching out of her subconscious. *The careening car. Screeching brakes. Hairpin curves. Going over the side!*

"What is it?" Jarrett stopped in the middle of the road and pulled her close. "You're trembling. What's the matter?"

For a moment, she braced herself against the pull of the past, fixing her mind on the protective arms Jarrett had around her. Slowly she began to relax as nothing happened. The view out the window remained the same.

"Tell me—now," he ordered, turning her face toward his, searching her eyes, watching her chew her bottom lip.

Her voice was strained but steady. "That's the curve...where the accident happened."

"What accident?"

"The one that killed Dave and Carole Mitchell, Benny's parents. Their car went over the side."

He stared at her in disbelief. "Nearly thirty years ago?"

His tone should have stopped her but the story came pouring out. She told him about being in the back seat, behind the couple, as the Studebaker raced out of control. She described the screams, the horror as the car splintered the guardrail and exploded into flames in the chasm below. "It...it was awful." She closed her eyes, still hearing the shattering glass, the crumpling metal and fiery explosion.

He brushed back the hair from her sweating forehead. "When you have a nightmare, you don't fool around, do you? Yours are three-dimensional and in living color."

"I don't think it was a nightmare."

"Of course it was," he assured her. "What else could it be? Your subconscious made use of the data you'd picked up about the accident and gave it back to you in a wild nightmare. I'll bet you a hundred dollars that this isn't anywhere near the spot where the tragedy occurred. Your mind played a trick on you when we went around that curve. Dreams are notoriously unreliable," he chided.

Not the ones I've had about you. She looked at him and let her hand trace the familiar thrust of his chin. No, they weren't dreams. Memories. Her fingertips touched his mouth.

"Is that a smile I see?" He moved his mouth to kiss her hand. "Is everything all right now?"

She let out a deep breath, smiled and said what he wanted to hear. "I guess you're right. I've let the saga of the Mitchell family become too personal."

He started driving down the road again and she settled back against the seat, still entertaining a firm conviction. *That was the curve, I know it.*

Jarrett kept the conversation light and entertaining the rest of the way to Wolverton. He glanced at his watch as they reached the city limits. "Four o'clock. I didn't know it was so late. I hope Mr. Griffin is still around.''

As he pulled in front of the newspaper office, a Closed sign on the door was his answer. A somnolent emptiness permeated Main Street. The only collection of cars was around Nellie's Place.

"Maybe it's early happy hour," said Jarrett. "Shall we join the natives?''

He took Lynne's arm as they crossed the street and she enjoyed the way his body brushed against hers in a casual but intimate way. They could hear music and smell hot grease even before they reached the restaurant. Something in the way Jarrett approached the door told her he'd been there before. She didn't know why that suspicion startled her. He could have stopped here on any of his trips to White Springs. She swallowed back an impulse to ask him.

Lynne could have sworn that half of the town was crammed into the smoky, dimly lighted room. Drinkers were standing two-deep at the bar. All the tables were filled and people were hanging out of booths as if there were a contest to see how many they could squeeze in. Raucous laughter and the blare of canned music came at Lynne with the force of a stereo turned up full blast. She would have turned and fled if Jarrett's hand hadn't been firmly on her arm.

They had only taken a couple of steps into the fray when a dark form rose up in front of her, blocking their way. In the murky light, his face was in shadow and it was a moment before she recognized the dark beard and craggy face.

"Oh, Griff," she said in relief. "We were looking for you." Her voice was about three decibels louder than normal. Even then she wasn't sure she could make herself heard above the bedlam. "This is Jarrett Taylor. He'd like to talk with you."

Maybe it was her imagination but the noise level around them seemed to go down as Griff barked, "What about?"

"Can we find a table?" Jarrett responded smoothly.

Griff hesitated and then gave a jerk of his head. He turned around and they followed his broad back. He headed toward the rear, down a back hall that offered Bull and Heifer restrooms. For a minute, Lynne thought the two men were going to disappear through the appropriate door and leave her in the hall, but Griff opened a door at the far end that led to a room filled with card tables. Apparently it was a little early in the day for poker because only one card game was in progress. Griff led them to a table against the wall.

Jarrett pulled out a chair for Lynne and eased down into one across from Griff. "Thanks for the rescue. That's something of a mob out there."

"Only decent place to get a drink anymore. Used to be a half dozen, but all the other places closed up." He peered at Jarrett under his bushy eyebrows. "What do you want to talk to me about?"

"Just about the town in general."

Griff raised his hand to a barmaid who came in with a tray of drinks for the card players. She looked like a high school girl dressed in jeans and sweatshirt and Lynne didn't think her old enough to be serving drinks.

Griff ordered a pitcher of beer and Jarrett paid for it. The newspaperman filled his mug up twice before he started responding to Jarrett's "as one man to another" chitchat.

Lynne was amused to see the way Jarrett defused Griff's reticence by playing up to the man's obvious territorial feeling about the area.

"Wolverton is a has-been town...not once but twice," said Griff in a lecturing tone. "It was a boomtown when prospectors poured into the Sawtooth Mountains looking for gold. Even though there were mines all over the place, nobody hit much of a bonanza. Production was modest and finally petered out. End of Wolverton's prosperity." He wiped the beer foam off his beard with his sleeve. "The place settled down into a quiet mountain community, attracting people like Benjamin, who had enough income to live where he wanted. He loved this place."

"What about his son?" Lynne asked, ignoring Jarrett's warning look.

"There was talk that Benjamin was going to build some sawmills between here and Silver City and put his son, Dave, in charge, but he was killed before anything happened. After Benjamin married Varina, the old guy didn't seem to be much interested in anything but his new wife and his grandson. Spent his time hunting and fishing. Didn't care that Wolverton was dying inch by inch."

"But Varina did?" Lynne asked casually. *Did the two of you share the same concerns?* Lynne wanted to ask how much influence Griff had had on the young widow after her husband's death.

Griff seemed to read her mind. "Varina's always been her own woman," he said flatly. "She saw the potential for this area becoming another Vail or Aspen. The Conifer Ridge Ski Resort lived up to its expectations just long enough for people to sink everything into building up Wolverton again. Varina did her best to keep the resort afloat, sank all the money she'd made on land and every penny Ben had left her into it. Even though people blame her, it wasn't her fault the company went into bankruptcy."

"Maybe if she'd relied more heavily on the judgment of people who knew the ski industry, she could have avoided—"

Griff cut Jarrett off. "You mean let a bunch of city investors drain her dry?" Griff countered abruptly. "Same difference. She'd end up getting the shaft either way."

"Maybe not," Jarrett persisted. "A profitable enterprise would be a good thing for everyone . . . bring Wolverton back."

Griff gave an ugly snort. "You won't be able to peddle that crapola around here."

"I think I can," Jarrett said with a pugnacious jut to his chin.

Griff shoved back his chair and stood up. All signs of friendliness vanished. His bulk and glowering expression cast a shadow as he leaned forward and banged one of his mammoth fists on the table. "I'll use whatever influence to stop Wolverton from being exploited by you or anyone else.''

"What about Varina?" Lynne foolishly baited. "She seems to be very excited about the prospect of new investors.''

"Then she's more of a fool than I thought.'' The lips above his black beard twisted in a snarl. He turned and stalked out of the room.

"Quite the chamber of commerce, isn't he?'' said Jarrett dryly.

Lynne suppressed a shiver. "He isn't putting out any welcome mat, that's for sure. I can't figure him out. In some ways, he seems very protective of Varina, and yet I have the feeling that he holds as much antagonism toward her as anyone else.''

"Maybe you're right. Maybe he is suffering from unrequited love. I wonder if Varina really did turn him down for the older, wealthier Benjamin Mitchell.''

A coarse laugh behind them jerked their heads around. Nellie stood a few feet away, taking off her jacket. Apparently she'd come in through a back door and Lynne wondered how long she'd been listening to their conversation.

CHAPTER ELEVEN

Jarrett shot a quick glance at Lynne and then looked over her shoulder and smiled. "Hi, Nellie. Nice to see you again."

That answered one question, thought Lynne. *Jarrett had been in the café before.*

Nellie sauntered over to their table wearing tight fuchsia stretch pants and a T-shirt with an announcement printed across her full breasts, Look But Don't Touch. Long earrings flipped around her full cheeks like dangling gold spaghetti.

"Well now, if it ain't slumming time for big city folk. I told you the other day, Mr. Whatever-your-name-is, that you could take your questions and—"

"Yes, I remember," Jarrett said, grinning. "You were very graphic. I enjoy your sense of humor, Nellie, and I like a lady who calls it as she sees it—even if she's wrong."

"What makes you think I'm wrong about a snoopin' speculator asking a lot of questions about people that are none of his dern business? I saw Griff stomping out of here. You two better keep your noses clean or he'll wipe them for you—get me?"

"Not really." Jarrett gave her a frank look. "What's going on? I would think the editor of a newspaper would want to promote the community—not try to hold it back.''

"You're way off, mister."

"Then show me the way," he challenged.

She gave a toss of her frizzy gray blond hair and shrugged. "Even if I knew, I wouldn't be spouting off to a couple of strangers." She picked up the pitcher of beer Griff had nearly emptied. She ignored Lynne completely. "You drinking or just passing the time of day?" she demanded of Jarrett.

"Glad you asked," he responded lightly. "We're drinking...and eating. Bring us a couple of steak sandwiches, fries and plenty of barbecue sauce." He gave her a suggestive grin. "You know, good and hot."

Her stiffness evaporated with a full and bawdy laugh. She winked at him. "Honey, you don't know what hot is!" With that, she turned and treated him to a suggestive swagger of her hips that brought a blush of color up into Lynne's cheeks.

Jarrett only laughed as she left the room. Lynne couldn't help but admire the way he had handled her. He'd established the kind of rapport that would probably make her greet him like an old customer. *The next time.*

"You've been in here before."

He nodded. "The first day when I was hunting a place to stay. I didn't realize how deep the rancor went. I was glad when I learned about the Mitchell house."

"I'm surprised anyone mentioned it. Varina said it hadn't been a B and B since her husband died." Once again, Lynne had an intuitive feeling that he wasn't telling her everything. *Maybe he had planned to stay at the house all along.* Had he been drawn to it the same way she had?

"Now you're looking at me with piercing gray eyes again. You're not sorry I showed up asking for a room, are you?"

"No, but—"

"But what?"

She bit her lower lip. "I just have the feeling you're not telling me everything."

His eyes sobered. "Funny. I have the same feeling about you."

Their eyes held for a long moment. He reached over and took her hand. "We found each other—that's all that matters, isn't it?"

The pressure of his warm clasp dissolved her nagging uneasiness. "Yes . . . that's all that matters."

The steak sandwiches were delicious and once again Jarrett proved he could be an entertaining dinner partner. All of her uneasiness vanished, and Lynne even smiled at Nellie when Jarrett paid the bill. He gave the woman a flirtatious smile. "See you later, Nellie."

Her bawdy laugh followed them out the door.

The house waited for them in the moonlight. As they entered the darkened front hall, she felt the present, past and maybe even the future all carefully balanced within its walls.

They slept in the small downstairs bedroom again, and even though the delight of making love was as strong as ever, Lynne experienced a vague disquiet that was like the far-off rumbling of an approaching storm. She clung to him as if he might disappear into a vaporous mist at any moment and she would never see him again. Her hands stroked the hard muscular sinews of his shoulders, his waist and thighs, her senses greedily absorbing every essence of his being. She delighted in the reality of his body surging in rhythm with hers, trying to hold back the moment of wild exploding sensation. Once their passion was spent, would her joy only be an echo in her own mind?

"Why are you crying?" he asked with concern, and kissed her moist eyelids.

She fought an insidious presentiment that this might be the last time they were together. *What if she lost him to another vivid memory—and nothing else?* At any moment wind rushing through a time tunnel might sweep him away from her.

"Sweet dreams," he whispered, drawing her close, and in a few moments his rhythmic breathing told her he was asleep. She rested her cheek against his chest, reassured by the warmth and the steady beat of his heart. She lay awake for a long time in the circle of his arms, keeping a vigil. Finally she drifted off into an uneasy sleep. And when she awoke the next morning, the same sense of disquiet was with her.

He waited until breakfast before telling her that he had to go to Denver to meet with some U.S. Forestry officials.

"That's a five-hour drive."

"I know. I've been putting it off but I have to find out if the government will grant another permit for this area. Environmentalists may have decided that enough land in Colorado has been leased to ski corporations. If that's the case, the Conifer Ridge investment scheme is down the drain. My appointment is for tomorrow morning. If all goes well, I'll start back after lunch tomorrow afternoon." He frowned like an anxious parent who was leaving a helpless child. "Maybe I shouldn't leave you alone."

If he'd used a different tone, Lynne probably would have suggested that she go along just to be with him on the long ride, but the implication that she couldn't manage by herself sparked an instant refusal. She used her professional tone. "I'm perfectly capable of taking care of myself. After all, I came here for some quiet renewal time. You go take care of your business. Don't worry about me. I assure you that—"

The phone rang.

"I'll get it," he said, getting up.

Lynne poured herself another cup of coffee. *He'll be back tomorrow.* There was absolutely no cause for the depression and sense of loneliness that were already creeping over her. No reason for the feeling of dread. Besides, she had never been dependent on others to fill up her life. Dixie had always complained she was the most solitary gal she'd ever known . . . perfectly happy to stay at home and enjoy her own company. Jarrett had changed all that, Lynne admitted as she waited for him to come back into the kitchen. Even though he was only a few rooms away, she wanted to give in and make some excuse to be with him.

She could hear his muffled voice as he engaged someone in a rather lengthy phone conversation. She set down her cup with a decisive click. Maybe she would go to Denver with him after all. He hadn't actually asked her to go, but even if he didn't have time for her in Denver, the long drive both ways would give them a chance to talk and enjoy each other's company. Why let pride deprive her of an exciting outing with the man she loved? She smiled at him when he came back into the kitchen but she didn't have a chance to tell him that she'd changed her mind.

"You'll never believe who that was—Varina Mitchell," he told her. "She's flying into Denver late this afternoon. Apparently her lawyer told her she ought to meet me. I could tell from the things she said that she's anxious to make sure my report is a positive one."

The look in his eyes was miles away. Lynne could almost see his mind clicking off business details that could be clarified in conversation with Varina. "I'm going to meet her at the Airport Stratton Hotel." He glanced at his watch as if calculating time and driving distance.

"Is she coming back here . . . to the house?"

He nodded. "She said she was sure you wouldn't mind her short visit."

"And what if I do?" Lynne bristled.

He looked at her in surprise. "Why would you? You've been wanting to get the lowdown on the Mitchell family—here's your chance." There was a suppressed excitement in his tone that unsettled her. Why was he glad to have someone else in the house? Could it be that he wanted to defuse the situation between them? Had she been too bold last night as she tried to hold on to the reality of his presence?

"She's breaking our agreement," Lynne said defensively. "We signed papers to give up our residences to each other for a period of four weeks."

"I know, but Varina indicated that you had already broken the agreement by allowing me to rent a room."

"But she gave permission!"

"In writing?"

"No, over the phone," snapped Lynne, glaring at him. "Is she planning on taking back her house?" Her hands were suddenly clenched.

"She didn't say that she was moving back," Jarrett assured her. "Just a short visit, I think. She said she wanted to be available to answer any of my questions. Obviously, she wants my investors to take over the bankrupt resort. You can't blame her for taking a personal interest in my recommendation."

His reasonable argument did nothing to lessen the upheaval she felt at the prospect of being displaced by the house's owner. And she already felt Jarrett slipping away from her.

"It's going to be all right." He put his hands on her shoulders, bent his head and nuzzled the back of her neck. "Maybe talking to Varina will lay to rest all your preoccupation with the past." He pulled her gently to her feet and searched her face. "I don't know what's worrying you. Varina seems like a reasonable person.

You'll work things out. As far as our relationship is concerned, she'll understand the situation."

How can she—when I don't understand it myself?

His thumb softly stroked the corners of her mouth. "Come on, relax." There was an edge to his voice that might have been irritation or worry. "Maybe we should let things cool down a bit."

"Cool down? Is that an euphemism for 'it's been fun, see you around sometime?'" She kept her tone light even as a tightness crept up in her throat.

He didn't answer for a moment and then he said, "I just meant that we need some time...to think clearly."

She'd watched him pack, encouraged a goodbye kiss and had forced a smile on her face as he'd driven away. The day was gray and gloomy, a match for her spirits, and she wasn't surprised when she looked out the kitchen window and saw snowflakes falling in thickening waves. An unreasonable panic seized her. What if she was pulled into more memories of skiing Buttermilk Run? Even though Jarrett had said that trail was one he had marked for the future, she still felt she had already skied down that slope in the past.

She turned away from the window, pressing her fingertips against her temples. All of her transcendental experiences seemed to be tied in some fashion to the house. The energy of ghostly spirits who had lived within its walls had repeatedly drawn her into a bewildering awareness of them. She had seen room furnishings change in color and content. A sense of urgency had reached out to her that lacked any comprehensible foundation in the present. The clue for understanding what was happening to her must lie within the walls of the old Victorian house and the people who had lived in it.

Armed with a new sense of purpose, she sat down at the kitchen table and went through the box of photographs again. As she stared at each photo, she tried to draw some psychic intuitions from it. She even closed her eyes and ran her fingers over the faded prints. The only thing that came to her was a feeling of utter foolishness.

Closing up the box, she took it back to the library and tried to put it in a desk drawer, where Jarrett had said he'd found it, but it wouldn't fit. He hadn't told her the truth; the box had come from someplace else.

Impulsively, Lynne went through the rest of the desk drawers even though her conscience protested, but she didn't find anything more of interest. Varina had cleaned them out except for things like pencils, notepads, paper clips and an assortment of pens. She shut the drawers and began checking the bookshelves for any old journals, albums or newspapers. Nothing.

Discouraged, she brushed back her hair, leaving a streak of dust across her cheek. Driven by a need to keep looking, she said aloud, "The attic."

As she climbed the stairs to the second floor, she remembered Jarrett's eagerness to check out the attic that first day, and again that night when he had slipped quietly past her room to open the attic door. That was where he had found the box of pictures. She was sure of it.

The attic stairs were narrow and dark and she scolded herself for not bringing a flashlight. Three dusty dormer windows provided enough light to see the usual attic clutter of discarded furniture, stacked boxes, old trunks, lamps and even a dressmaker's dummy.

She stood in the midst of the assorted junk and tried to come up with some idea of what she was looking for. The trunks were empty...a disappointment. She'd half expected them to be filled with exciting memorabilia. As she looked around and poked through boxes, she couldn't see anything that would interest a second-hand dealer, let alone anything that helped her understand the "time" confusion she'd experienced since she entered the house. If there had been any antiques stored in the attic, they were gone now. She wondered where Jarrett had found the box of pictures. The question suddenly filled her mind with new suspicion. Was that the only thing he'd found? What else was he keeping from her?

She turned around, went down the stairs and walked purposefully through the house. His small room showed evidence of hurried packing. The bed was in the same tumbled state as when they'd crawled out of it, and the scent of their warm bodies lingered in the air. His presence was so strong that she faltered in her impulse to search the room. The energy that had propelled her all morning dissipated. With wooden movements, she made the bed. Then she sat down on it and stared unseeing at the wall in front of her.

Trust me.

There had been a gentle pleading in his words and a promise that he would be there for her. But there had been something else, too. A withholding. A hidden purpose that he wasn't willing to share.

She sighed deeply, stood up and walked back to the gloomy kitchen. Lowering storm clouds blanketed the sun and snow whipped against the window, piling up on the window ledge and coating the glass. Was it going to be a blizzard? Surely not the first snow of the season, she reasoned. As she listened to the soft sweep of snow piling up around the house, she realized how lonely it must have been for Varina living in this deserted mountain valley, especially after the colorful, vigorous activity of a ski resort. No wonder she was anxious to do whatever she could to bring back those days. Varina must have stubbornly held on to the house with the hope that someday the bankrupt company would find new financing and start up again. Lynne could sympathize with the disappointments she must have experienced living alone, treated badly by the townspeople. Maybe Griff had been the only one to remain her greatest friend. *Or enemy.*

Lynne fixed a cup of soup and a sandwich and went into the library to eat her lunch in front of the fire. Drowsy contentment came over her but she guarded against falling asleep, fearful that another nightmare might overtake her. Bored with the novel that she'd started several times, she opened one of the glass-fronted bookcases and took out a book about an English lady traveling alone by horseback in Colorado in the winter of 1873. The account kept her interested and she read for nearly an hour before her eyelids suddenly became heavy. Intending to close them for only a moment, she leaned her head back in the chair.

The sound of something falling woke her. She jerked up, her heart racing. For a moment, she couldn't move. Slowly she let her eyes rove around the room, expecting to find herself transported into another time dimension. Everything was the same. She looked on the floor and saw that her book had fallen off her lap. A giddy feeling of relief swept over her. When she dozed off for a moment, the book must have slipped out of her hand.

The fire had died down and she reached for a log just as the flicker of movement across the marble front of the fireplace drew her head around. Like a shadow on the wall, she glimpsed the figure of the little boy scooting out of the room.

"Wait."

She bounded to the door and looked up and down the hall.

It was empty.

Lynne went slowly back into the library. Instead of being upset by the incident, she acknowledged the warmth that always accompanied the little boy's appearance. A strange bond stretched between them and she'd been unable to break it even when terror had driven her out of the house. Some inexplicable force seemed to be reaching out to hold her firmly to a commitment she didn't understand. She only knew that a moment ago she had glimpsed the dead child's presence.

I must have been asleep longer than it seemed, she thought. The fire had almost burned out. As she re-kindled the flames, an eerie moaning came down the chimney. She threw on an extra log and then walked to the window. Easing back the edge of the drape, she peered out and squinted against a pristine whiteness from blowing gusts of swirling flakes. Drifts were already piling up against the house.

Her chest tightened. What if the storm closed all the roads? And the telephone lines went down? Her nails bit into her flesh as she stood there and knew with strange certainty that her isolation was about to become complete.

CHAPTER TWELVE

The storm raged against the house like a demented creature, throwing snow against the windows and wailing down the chimneys. Trees bending in the onslaught of the wind sent needle-laden branches writhing against the outside walls and roof. She couldn't see anything but darkness beyond the swirls of snowflakes that blotted out the landscape.

The telephone rang just as she turned back to the fire. *Jarrett!* She grabbed it with a breathless and hopeful, "Hello."

"Hi, sweetheart. Been worried about you. How's the weather?"

"It's snowing hard."

"According to the news the northern mountains are really socked in. Are you all right?"

"I am now," she said honestly. "I've been suffering withdrawal symptoms. Needed to hear your voice. It seems like a long time since this morning."

"I know. All the way to Denver I wished you hadn't been so adamant about not coming."

I changed my mind but it was too late. "Have you seen Varina yet?"

"No, she hasn't checked in yet but we'll probably have dinner. The Forest Service was pretty optimistic about issuing a new permit for an adequately financed operation. I'm eager to get some firsthand information from her."

"What time will you be back tomorrow?"

He hesitated. "Hard to say, with the storm and all."

She had the feeling that he was hedging on his promise to return as planned. She said crisply, "Of course, you will want to see how the roads are."

"You know I'll come as soon as I can."

Do I? Then she took herself in hand. "I'll be fine. Just think of me sitting in front of the fire, practicing my shell-spitting shots."

He laughed. "No fair." His tone softened. "I miss you, darling. How can I expect to get any sleep in this king-size hotel bed? No elbows in my face... no knees in my stomach?"

She teased him that he was the one who insisted on sleeping cupped together like two spoons. The exchange of intimate barbs brought remembered warmth and desire and his voice was husky as he said, "I'd better hang up before I get in my car and start back tonight."

They delayed saying goodbye for several minutes, with the dallying procrastination of lovers, and when Lynne put down the receiver, she fought the urge to call him right back.

His call left her with a warm feeling, which was a good thing because the house grew colder as the storm outside raged. She put on an extra sweater and stayed near the fire in the library, eating and reading. The account of Isabella Bird's travels was entertaining enough to hold her attention until the lights began to flicker, threatening to plunge the house into total darkness at any moment.

Throwing down the book, she hurriedly crossed the hall to the dining room. The candelabra that Jarrett had used the night they had dinner was still on the table. The five white candles were about half consumed. Lynne found the matches just as the lights went out.

The sudden darkness brought a tightening in her stomach and a trembling to her hands. The house was alive with a cacophony of groans and moans as the roof, windows and doors were assaulted by high winds and raging snow. Thank goodness she'd found the candles. She only lit three of them, unsure if there were more in any of the drawers.

Bathed in an eerie circle of light, she moved across the dark hall and back into the library. She set the candelabra on the desk beside the telephone. The need for human contact was so great that she reached for the phone and impulsively dialed Dixie's office number. Even with an hour's time difference, she should still be there, Lynne reasoned.

"Social Services. Dixie Witherspoon speaking."

"Hi, Dixie. Working hard?" Lynne's grip on the receiver eased at the sound of Dixie's Southern drawl.

"Well, if it isn't our lady of leisure—calling to gloat, no doubt," her friend chided her with a chuckle in her voice. "You must have known I was cussing you out this morning. I found a bunch of your cases in my intake basket. Was tempted to call you but decided I shouldn't intrude. I mean, you seemed pretty well preoccupied with the love of your life the last time we talked. Everything's still hot, isn't it?''

Lynne thought about last night's passionate love-making and laughed sheepishly. "Real hot. But Jarrett's in Denver on business. He'll be gone until tomorrow. It's snowing hard and I thought I'd better call before the lines go down."

"You mean there's a chance you'll be snowed in that old house—all by yourself?"

Not exactly all by myself. She wanted to tell Dixie about the haunting of the house but knew that her friend would really go into a panic. She changed the subject. "I may be back in Chicago before you know it. Varina Mitchell called this morning...she made arrangements to meet Jarrett in Denver. Apparently she intends to put pressure on him to deliver a positive report to his investors about putting the bankrupt resort back into business. Anyway, she's coming back to the house with him tomorrow."

"Can she do that? Move back while you're still there?"

"Not according to our signed agreement." Lynne sighed. "She told Jarrett I had already broken the contract by letting him have a room."

"I thought you got permission?"

"I did, but it was only verbal."

There was a silence and then Dixie said firmly, "You're better off to pack your bags and come home. Maybe touch base with somebody else in another part of the country if you're still in the mood to swap houses."

Dixie made it sound so easy. No problem at all. Just go back to Chicago and her work, pick up her empty life and chalk up the Colorado house-swapping experience to bad judgment. How could she begin to explain the strange attraction that had brought her to the Mitchell house in the first place and the unseen forces that kept her there? And what about Jarrett? "I can't leave . . . not yet."

"Why not? What's holding you? If that handsome houseguest of yours loses interest because you come back home, you're better off without him. I say hand the house keys to Mrs. Mitchell and get the heck out of there." Dixie softened her tone. "I don't understand why you'd want to stay."

Lynne was silent, accepting the truth. *I don't understand the reason, either.* Aloud, she said, "I'll make my decision after I talk with Varina. Maybe she has no intention of being here more than a few days. Jarrett is almost finished with his report and . . . and . . ."

"And what? Does he have any plans . . . about you, I mean?"

"I don't know. We haven't talked about it."

Dixie gave an explosive release of air. "If you love him as much as you say, you'd better find out what kind of signposts he's putting up. Dead End or Straight Ahead."

Lynne laughed. Leave it to Dixie to want everything in bold print. "There are lots of things we haven't talked about," she admitted. Uncertainty crept into her voice. "We really haven't had time to discuss everything."

"You sure he's not already married?"

"I'm sure." Lynne didn't know why, but she had every confidence that what Jarrett had told her about his private life was true. He was a bachelor, living in his hometown of Santa Fe, New Mexico, and he'd come to Colorado on business. She knew how hard he'd been working for his client and she didn't doubt that he had her welfare at heart.

"He's not everything he appears to be, is that it?"

"Of course he is!" she countered defensively.

"Then what is it?" Dixie prodded. "Listen, gal, I can tell when you're not satisfied with a situation. Heaven knows, I've watched you hunt, dig and search like a bloodhound when you were convinced you didn't have the right information on a case. You've got that same tone in your voice now. There's something about Prince Charming that's worrying you."

Lynne couldn't explain her nagging suspicion that Jarrett was hiding something from her. If she told Dixie about the box of photos hidden under his bed, she'd have to admit to her fascination with the Mitchell family and Jarrett's reasoning that she was already suffering from a fixation on the past. Then she'd have to tell Dixie about the nightmares and her friend would really worry that she'd lost her mind. Better to lie. She gave an amused laugh. "You're way off, Dixie. I'm not worried about a thing."

"You just call me at the office to tell me you're not worried about a thing? Get real, kiddo. You're uptight and you know it."

"Well, maybe a little. We're in the midst of a snow-storm and the lights just went out."

"Heaven help us! Have you reported it?"

"Yes," Lynne lied, not wanting to admit she hadn't done any such thing. She'd just assumed the outage would be noticed by someone—foolish thought. "I'm fine. No reason to panic," she said, as much for her own benefit as Dixie's. "After all, I knew what to expect from Colorado winters—"

"I don't think you did," Dixie countered. "Once you saw the photograph of that Victorian house, you set your mind like a mule hunkered down in the middle of the road. Nothing was going to change your mind. You wouldn't even listen to reason."

"Okay, okay. I gave in to an emotional impulse, but maybe I didn't have a choice."

"Now what is tarnation do you mean by that? Of course you had a choice. You're not going to hit me with any of that predestiny stuff, are you? That high altitude must be depriving you of enough oxygen to think clearly. You'd better get off that mountain and get back to reality."

Reality? Lynne wasn't certain she could define its limits anymore. Since her arrival at the house, she'd been swept in and out of the present with bewildering reality. The experiences she'd had in the past had been as sharp and clear as any of the moment. And the memories of Jarrett were undeniable.

She changed the subject and engaged Dixie in some office chitchat. After a few assurances that she'd stay warm and dry, Lynne hung up, a little annoyed with herself for having called Dixie in the first place. Not being perfectly candid had put a strain on their friendship. How could Dixie possibly understand all the turns her life had taken?

She searched for a telephone directory in vain. She'd have to call information and get the number for the electric company servicing the area. Before she could reach for the phone again, there was a loud crash of something falling against the house. The noise vibrated through the library and a rush of air sent smoke down the chimney. The room was filled with a billowing black cloud.

Coughing, Lynne turned her back to the fireplace and covered her nose with her hands. The blast of smoke dissipated enough for her to grab the phone. She bounced the receiver knob.

Nothing. The phone was dead.

Her eyes smarted from the smoke and she let a rush of tears flow down her cheeks as she hung up the phone. The sound of the wind had changed to laughter. The house joined in the macabre onslaught of her senses. As she stood in the uncertain candlelight, her ears were filled with the storm's manic raving. Darkness stretched away to the haunting depths of the house and the acrid odor of smoke filled her nostrils and caused a burning in her chest.

She stood there for a long moment before she brushed a hand across her wet cheeks, picked up the candles and slowly mounted the stairs. Shadows like ghostly specters dogged her footsteps as she went into her bedroom. She knew there would be no heat until the electricity came back on and she was already shivering in the invading chill. There was only one place in the house that offered warmth and reassurance. She'd spend the night in Jarrett's room, huddled in the bed where his loving presence would be felt.

The battering of the storm was even louder on the second floor. She hurriedly collected her warmest nightgown, a quilted robe and thick knee-high socks. The weak candlelight cast an eerie patina on the walls, and her hasty movements were reflected in the mirror, which seemed to taunt her as light and dark shadows played across its silvered surface.

She refused to give in to the mounting sense of menace. The house must have endured many storms like this, she told herself nervously as she gathered up things. Jarrett would be back tomorrow, she reassured herself stubbornly. The storm would blow itself out and by this time tomorrow night they'd be curled up together in his narrow bed.

Clutching her clothes in one hand and holding the candelabra in the other, she started down the second-floor hall. A high-pitched wailing made her head jerk up. Babies crying?

Holding the candles forward, she stopped in the doorway of the next bedroom and stared into it as light flickered over its Early American furnishings. She had been drawn to this room once before, the night Jarrett had gone to the attic, but she couldn't remember why. She was certain that the whimpering sounds were coming from the deserted room. But there was nothing there. As she stood there, a vaporous vision hovered just beyond her memory. She tried to draw it forth but it slithered away like gray mist. Her ears strained to hear the sound again but only the noise of whipping snow and howling wind echoed through the room.

She turned away and walked back to the stairs. It must have been the wind making a crying sound. She marched down the steps and along the dark hall to the back room with an anxious impatience, as if ready to do battle with taunting forces within the house.

She tossed her clothes on the bed and made room for the large candelabra on the dresser. And that's when she found the photograph. At first she thought it was one from the old box, but even in the yellow candlelight she could tell that it wasn't one she'd seen before. She turned it over and read the scribbled writing on the back.

Dismay shot through her. Her body was suddenly encased in a hot sweat. There must be some mistake. Some explanation. Her thoughts whirled like dry leaves caught in a devil's wind. It couldn't be.

She picked up the candelabra and made her way through the dark kitchen and down the hall to the library. Placing the flickering candles on the desk, she brought the box of old photos close to the light. Her trembling fingers quickly found the photo she was looking for. She laid it side by side with the one she'd found on the dresser. They were almost identical. The same little boy grinned at the camera in both photos.

Lynne turned over the one she'd just found. Someone had written on the back. Jarrett Taylor. 340 Cactus Drive. Santa Fe, New Mexico.

CHAPTER THIRTEEN

Lynne felt the darkened house closing in on her. For a moment she couldn't breathe. The two photographs glowed with a hypnotic sheen as she stared at them. The resemblance of the little boy with his teddy bear to the grinning child identified as Jarrett Taylor was undeniable. This new revelation defied all logic. *Had the spirit of the dead boy become fused with a mortal man who had become her lover? Or were they both phantoms of her mind?* A bone-shaking chill invaded her body. Where did reality end . . . and madness begin?

Gusts of wind rattling the house rose in loud laughter as she stood there trembling. The house no longer seemed empty but filled with unseen specters crowding into the shadows of the room. A high-pitched whine like that of a hundred wings whipping the air filled her ears. *What do you want from me?* The anguished cry came deep from within.

She stumbled from the library, holding the candelabra in front of her. The candles threatened to blow out as she bounded through the dark kitchen and down the back hall. She slammed the bedroom door shut. With a gasp, she put the candles on the floor. Fully dressed, she burrowed down in the bed covers like a hunted animal seeking warmth and safety.

Her breath came in short heaves. She closed her eyes tightly as if to shut out any apparitions that dared assault her. Even if she felt moist mist upon her face, she wouldn't open them. *Leave me alone.* She sobbed, knowing that the man she loved was a part of the time warp that had engulfed her.

Sometime during the night, the candles burned out, the wind died down and she fell into a fitful sleep.

A hushed silence greeted Lynne as she stirred in the morning light; she felt relaxed at first, then awareness and memory dispelled the lassitude of sleep. For a moment she just lay there, unwilling to handle the trauma that had engulfed her the night before. Had she experienced another nightmare? She wasn't certain anymore that her grasp of time and reality were reliable. She could have fallen asleep and dreamed last night's trauma. And the matching photographs could have been part of it.

She could hear the furnace running. The house felt warm. Yes, that must be it, she thought with relief. Everything had been an aberration. The snow...the power outage...and the photograph. All of it had happened in one of her "nightmares."

She sat up. A smell of wax brought her eyes to the candelabra sitting beside the bed. Burnt candles were only nubs of wax. She turned her head and saw that her nightclothes were still piled at the foot of the bed. Slowly her gaze went to the small window. The drawn shade didn't quite cover all the glass and revealed a ribbon of snow pressed against the pane.

Her throat was suddenly dry. The storm had been real enough. What about the rest of it? A dull headache sharpened as she got to her feet and walked purposefully through the house to the library. She touched the light switch and the light came on.

The two photos lay where she had left them on the table. In the bright glare of electric lights, the resemblance seemed even more marked than she had remembered. With detached calmness, she put both photos in the box and shut the lid. With a firm jut to her chin, she picked up the dangling receiver, ready to call Jarrett at the hotel number he'd left.

No dial tone. The phone outage had not been a dream. She was without a phone.

Pulling back the heavy window drapes, she looked out on a serene mountain landscape covered with silver-speckled snow. A few lingering clouds spread across a penetrating blue sky but the first storm of the season was over. Everything looked deceptively soft. Even the ugly cluster of buildings were mounds of sculptured snow. The wild fury of last night's storm was a sharp contrast to the hushed silence that lay upon the scene. The unearthly quiet in the house was as harsh on Lynne's nerves as a jangle of noise would have been. *Jarrett. Jarrett.* Was he slipping away just like all the other shadowy presences she'd glimpsed in the house? She sensed that the past and the present were merging into one thin line—stretching away from her into some undefinable point beyond her consciousness.

She turned away from the window and went upstairs. She made as much noise as she could running her bath, opening and shutting drawers and walking firmly around her bedroom and down the stairs. A foolish defiance. A declaration. *He's real. You can't take him from me!*

She spent nearly an hour making up a batch of bran muffins and fixing a Spanish omelet that would have fed six. Furious physical activity kept her thoughts in neutral. She carried in more wood and vigorously mopped the kitchen floor where her boots had left snow tracks.

She was reorganizing a pantry shelf to see what canned food was left when she heard the front doorbell. With joy she wouldn't have thought possible, she raced to open it.

"Griff!" He could have been an IRS auditor and she would have welcomed him with open arms. "Come in. Come in. What a nice surprise. I just took some muffins out of the oven and I have a pot of coffee waiting." She knew she was blabbering but she couldn't help it. "Here, let me take your coat. The roads are open, then?"

He wiggled out of a heavy mackinaw and took off his stocking cap and smoothed his beard. "Yeah, they're okay. Not much of a storm. Mostly blowing snow. About six inches accumulation. Got the telephone lines, though." He peered at her from under his bushy eyebrows. "Cliff Brown at the gas station said that city fellow filled up on his way to Denver yesterday. Thought I'd better check in . . . just to make sure you weathered the storm all right."

She smiled at him gratefully. "The electricity went out . . . left me in the dark for a while." In other circumstances she might have questioned his neighborly interest, but her joy at having someone break the brooding silence of the house won out over any skepticism that he was behaving out of character. "Come have a cup of coffee with me."

The next hour passed pleasantly as the topics of conversation moved from Colorado winters to the book she'd been reading about the Englishwoman's travels in the Rockies. Lulled by a sense of comradeship, Lynne brought the conversation around to the Mitchell family and impulsively decided to show him the two photographs. She handed them to him so he couldn't see what was written on the back of the one.

"You knew the Mitchell child. Would you say that both of these pictures are of the same little boy?"

Griff frowned, looking from one to the other. Then he nodded his shaggy head. "That's little Benny, all right."

Even though she had already been convinced in her own mind, she felt sick. The little boy who had been haunting her and the man she loved were somehow meshed together. One was a phantom appearing and disappearing in the house, and the other . . . ? Her mind faltered. If she walked out the door now, would she ever see Jarrett in the present again? Did her memories of him verify that he was a part of the past and nothing more?

She took the photos from Griff and walked over to the counter to give herself time to compose herself. Then she picked up the percolator and walked back to the table. "Benny loved his teddy bear, didn't he? How did it lose an ear?"

Griff's eyes narrowed. "How'd you know about that?"

"I...I must have noticed it in one of the photographs," she lied, sitting down and fingering her coffee cup. "There's a whole box of family photographs. I confess I've been looking through them. Quite a few of you," she said, wishing she'd never brought up the subject.

"Varina won't like it," he said flatly as he buttered another muffin. "She's a private person."

"I'll explain when she gets here. Jarrett is bringing her back from Denver. I expect them late this afternoon if the roads are open. Would you like more coffee?"

"Varina's coming back?" He stopped chewing.

Lynne nodded.

"But I thought you'd traded houses...for a month."

"We did."

"Why has she changed her mind?"

"She wants to meet Jarrett and try to influence the report he's going to make to the investors." Lynne mechanically took a sip of coffee. "Anyway, both of us have broken our written agreement, so I'll be going back to Chicago and she'll be free to stay in her own house."

The only thing she could tell from his expression was that he wasn't indifferent to Varina's return. Whether glad or sorry, she couldn't tell. Suddenly she felt uncomfortable in his presence. He hunched in his chair like a huge brooding animal. His hooded eyes were dark and expressionless. She wished he'd go.

"I'm through with the newspapers you loaned me. Just a minute and I'll get them from the library. I brought them with me the other day and didn't get a chance to give them to you."

He seemed to pick up on her uneasiness as she came back and handed him the newspapers. Thanking her for the coffee and muffins, he left as abruptly as he'd come. He'd been gone about twenty minutes when she discovered that both of the photographs were gone from the kitchen counter where she'd laid them when she served the coffee.

CHAPTER FOURTEEN

Jarrett and Varina arrived at the house about five that afternoon. The sun had already set behind the crystal-line peaks, and the valley lay in shadow except for lights from the house spilling out onto the snow. Lynne peered out the front window and could tell from the amount of luggage being unloaded from the car that Varina had come to stay.

She was a small, quick-moving woman with a pur-poseful stride. Her naturally silvered black hair had been cut in a simple shoulder length so that it framed alert blue eyes and well-balanced features. The mo-ment she entered the house, an energy like static elec-tricity snapped around her.

Varina grabbed Lynne's hand with a firm squeeze. "You must think I'm terribly brash coming back like this. I really must apologize. When I signed our agree-ment, I truly intended to spend the next month in and around Chicago. You understand, don't you? I've been waiting such a long time for someone to take an inter-est in Conifer Ridge—and now someone has!" She sent Jarrett a grateful smile as he came in with two of her suitcases. Then she swung her attention back to Lynne. "There's no question about it...I just have to be here." The firm set of her mouth added there was no room for negotiation. "Of course, you don't have to leave immediately."

"How hospitable of you," Lynne said dryly.

"Oh, dear, I hope you're not going to be difficult about this." She looked worried. "I know you must be terribly upset. We traded places in good faith but my future livelihood is at stake. I couldn't stay in Chicago. Not when there might be something I could do to get the resort back in operation. I sacrificed everything my husband had left me to develop the resort and make it a success. When it went bankrupt, I thought I'd die." There was a haunting pain in her eyes and Lynne suddenly felt sorry for her.

"I understand," she said. She could feel Varina's anxiety. The reason for her return was clear. With so much at stake, Lynne knew she would have done the same thing. "I hope it all works out for you."

"I've told her that I can't guarantee anything," Jarrett said as he set all of her suitcases on the bottom stair. "Things look promising but you never can tell about these things. It will take me a couple more days to finalize my report and then it's out of my hands."

And then what? Lynne sought the answer in his face. Was it a Dead End for them or Straight Ahead as Dixie had so aptly put it? She couldn't tell since he'd made no move to touch her or indicate in any way that there was anything intimate between them. In fact, a warning seemed to accompany a brief locking of his eyes with hers. Lynne didn't understand. They were both adults. There was no reason they had to be accountable to Varina just because she owned the house. Why didn't he want Varina to know that they cared for each other? *Something's changed.*

He was smiling at Varina. "If you'll show me which room is yours, I'll carry your bags up."

Hers is the locked bedroom at the end of the hall— and you know it! Lynne flared silently. What kind of game was he playing—and why? She watched the two of them go up the stairs together. Like someone looking through a murky window, she couldn't see clearly. She felt shut out.

Damn him, she swore, her lips trembling. Why couldn't he have taken her in his arms, dispelled the disquiet that had been growing with bewildering unanswered questions? No matter how bizarre her experiences had been, he had always been there, reassuring and protective. Even though she didn't understand it, she accepted the truth that she had known him before, and the one thing that had been consistent was a deep abiding love. But his cool, rather indifferent return had changed all that. With deadening certainty, she knew that he had slipped away from her. She was tempted to pack up her things and leave all the confusion and heartache behind, but something still held her back. With a deep sigh, she went into the kitchen and checked the three casseroles she'd put in the oven.

After she discovered Griff had taken the photos, her thoughts had been in such turmoil that she gave in to a fury of cooking that had lasted throughout the day. She depleted the refrigerator of anything that could be chopped, diced and sliced. She prepared several kinds of pasta and made up a cheese-and-tuna dish, chicken casserole and a concoction of green beans and Chinese noodles. She tried a variety of recipes offered on the back of a box of pancake mix. Not much was left in the cupboards or pantry when she finished, but somehow she'd made it through the day without having time for emotional upheavals. As she surveyed the offerings of her frantic cooking binge, she wanted to hide everything.

"What is all this?" Jarrett asked as he and Varina came in the kitchen.

"We brought steaks for supper," Varina said. "Thought it would be quick and easy." She eyed all the pasta dishes and her hands instinctively touched her flat stomach. "We didn't expect you to prepare...a smorgasbord."

"It's just a welcome-home feast," said Lynne, determined not to be cowed by Jarrett's raised eyebrows or Varina's appalled expression. "We can freeze most of it...so you'll have meals prepared ahead of time," Lynne said, improvising.

"That's...that's very thoughtful of you," Varina managed.

"She'll have enough for several months, I'd wager," Jarrett said dryly. "One person might not be able to eat all that before spring."

"Maybe she'll have company." Lynne's next remark wasn't all that innocent. "Griff was up here today and I told him Varina was coming home." She waited to see what Varina's reaction would be and wasn't disappointed. The color in the woman's face faded to ashen. *Varina's afraid of him.*

"What did he want?"

"Just checking...making sure I was all right. The telephone line is down."

"I know," said Jarrett. "I tried calling you late last night and this morning. The news reported a blizzard. I was afraid the roads might be closed today."

Her eyes met his with a silent message. *So was I.*

"How come Griff's taken you under his wing?" Varina demanded. Before Lynne could answer, Varina pursed her lips, then said, "He's probably just using you as an excuse to come snooping around. Never could mind his own business. That newspaper has been his excuse to poke his nose in everything. When Ben was alive, Griff was always pestering him to go fishing or hunting. After my husband died and I got the ski resort in operation, he practically lived at the lodge."

"Maybe he's sweet on you," Jarrett suggested, smiling. "You've known him for a long time, haven't you, Varina?"

"Before Ben and I were married," she admitted. "I don't think he was ever happy about the marriage, but I didn't care. I knew what I wanted in a man and Griff wasn't it. I'm sorry if he's been pestering you, Lynne."

Lynne hesitated to say that the newspaperman had made off with the photographs she'd showed him. Heaven knows what he intended to do with them. She wanted to talk to Jarrett about that...but not in Varina's presence.

It was obvious that Varina was now in charge. She took command of the kitchen, telling Jarrett where to put the groceries they'd brought and changing Lynne's arrangement of things on the counter. She decided they would eat in the kitchen instead of the dining room. "Too much fuss," she declared. "Besides, Jarrett, I want to go over some ledgers with you as soon as we've eaten."

Varina didn't wait until after dinner to monopolize the conversation. Lynne could have been sitting in some other part of the house as far as the woman was concerned. Jarrett listened attentively to everything she said and Lynne suppressed the urge to kick him under the table.

When Varina suggested coffee in the library because she wanted to see the projected plans Jarrett had prepared, Lynne finally conceded defeat. "I'll let you two see to business while I clean up."

Neither of them protested. A half hour later as she walked down the hall toward the library, she heard their voices raised in a heated discussion and they didn't even look up when she walked in. With a stubborn tilt to her chin she picked up her book, then turned and walked out again.

"Good night," Jarrett called after her. "Sweet dreams."

The tone of his voice seemed to hold a promise. *See you later.* As she prepared for bed, she took care to brush her hair until it shone, and touched a drop of perfume to her earlobes. Her gown had a lace-edged neckline and soft sleeves that draped prettily over her shoulders. *He would come.* Once the house was quiet and Varina was safely bedded down in her room, he would quietly mount the stairs. She gave the pillows a good thumping and folded down the covers on his side so he could easily slip in beside her.

She read for a while, one ear tuned for the sound of Varina coming upstairs to bed. Finally she put the book down, resigned that Varina wasn't going to call it an early night. No telling how long she'd keep Jarrett going over records and other data. Varina was one determined woman, thought Lynne.

She finally turned off her reading light and lay in the dark, thinking how good it would be to have Jarrett's warmth wrapped around her, to feel his lover's touch and delight in whispered endearments as his lips teased the soft valley of her neck and breasts. A desperate need to know that he cared about her brought tears to the corners of her eyes. His arms-length coolness had shaken her more than she wanted to admit.

At last, Varina came upstairs. Lynne listened to muffled sounds floating down the hall from Varina's room and bath. Then all was still. A hushed waiting became an eternity as the minutes ticked by...and then an hour. Another thirty minutes. *He's not coming.*

At last, she forced herself to face the truth. In contrast to her intense and deep feelings, he wanted to keep the relationship between them light and casual. He had warned her often enough by his controlled manner and unreadable thoughts, but she had refused to temper her feelings. What a fool she'd been. She should have known that such attractive, charming man would have enjoyed many romantic interludes and readily ended them when the time came. Her disappointment was suddenly laced with anger, at herself and at him. He had misled her. Played her on her emotions. Made a fool of her.

She flung off the covers and grabbed her robe and slippers. She had a few things to say before he sauntered out of her life and chalked Lynne Delevan as another conquest. Quietly opening her door, she slipped into the hall and down the stairs, grateful that the hall light illuminated most of the passage to the kitchen. A fire still glowed in the library but all the rooms on the first floor were deserted, dark and quiet.

She didn't turn on a light when she reached the kitchen but slowed her steps and carefully navigated around chairs in the dark, praying she wouldn't knock something over that would bring Varina running down the stairs.

As she reached the back hall, she saw a sliver of light coming from under Jarrett's door. Angrily she flung open his door, expecting to see him lying in bed waiting for her.

He wasn't there.

The caustic greeting she had formed on her lips faded. The bed was still made. There was no sign that he'd unpacked the suitcase that stood near the foot of the bed. Where was he? The door to the small bathroom across the hall was open. No Jarrett. She hesitated. Should she wait for him?

Her thoughts raced in several directions at once. He hadn't been in any of the rooms she'd passed. Had he come up the stairs—with Varina? No, she would have heard his footsteps. She would have known if there had been two people passing her door.

Slowly Lynne walked back to the kitchen. She flicked the light and saw that the room was just as she'd left it after dinner cleanup. She put a hand to her forehead and tried to think. Jarrett wasn't in any of the downstairs rooms. He hadn't come up to the second floor. Her head ached as she tried to figure where he could be. Could he have left the house at this hour? She swallowed back a spurt of anxiety. Why on earth would he do that? The night was cold and the ground was covered with snow. She would have heard his car if he had driven away.

She peered out the kitchen window, watching for any kind of movement, but the landscape remained serene and still. *Jarrett—where are you?*

She turned away from the window and noticed that the door leading to the basement was slightly ajar. Dank air rushed out at her as she pushed it further open. She flipped the light switch but nothing happened. Below, in the darkness, a moving circle of light suddenly bathed the wooden steps.

She saw Jarrett's face in the flashlight's illumination and his expression kept her from calling out to him. The skin on the back of her neck tightened. She'd never seen a grimace so tortured, so anguished, like someone writhing in hell. She must have gasped, for he suddenly looked up and saw her standing on the landing.

"What is it, Jarrett?"

His voice was guttural and strained as he whispered something deep in his throat.

CHAPTER FIFTEEN

"What is it? What did you find?" She grabbed his arm as he reached the top step and then closed the cellar door. "Jarrett! What is it?"

He passed a hand over his eyes. "I need a drink." She got the brandy and poured him a healthy amount. He took a swig and then shivered.

"Sit down," she ordered. Her own chest was tight. What had he found in the cellar? Taking the chair next to his, she gripped her hands tightly, holding back a barrage of questions. Had he found someone buried in the cellar? The macabre thought brought a bone-shaking chill.

She waited. After a few moments, the deep creases in his cheeks began to ease. He leaned back in the chair, faint color returning to his cheeks. Her patience ran out. "What were you doing in the cellar, Jarrett?"

His forehead furrowed. "I'm not quite sure. Looking for something . . . ?"

"And you found it?"

He gave her a perplexed look. "No."

"Then what?"

"I can't explain it. Something made me go down to the basement. It was as if I were hypnotized or under some kind of spell. And then something attacked me.

Something . . . nebulous . . . thick enough to choke me.
I couldn't move . . . it was like a nightmare." He stared
at her. "Nightmare! Is this the kind of thing that's been
happening to you?"

She nodded.

He grabbed her hands. "Until tonight I didn't realize what you've been going through. I'm so sorry,
Lynne. You tried to tell me but I didn't understand.
You've experienced the same kind of attack, haven't
you?" At her nod, he said gruffly, "You've got to
leave . . . get out of here."

"What about you?"

He shook his head. "I can't. I have to stay, but you
don't. Please, for heaven's sake, don't argue with me.
Whatever happens, I don't want you here."

"What is going to happen?" She searched his face
and saw a veil come over those dark blue eyes.

"I don't know."

He wasn't telling her the truth. He was keeping
something back. "Jarrett—"

"I want you to leave . . . right away . . . in the morning."

"Listen to me. While you were gone I found a photograph—"

A muffled sound turned their eyes to the doorway.
Varina stood there. Jarrett drew his hand away.

"My, my, I see I'm not the only one wanting a midnight snack." Varina eyed Jarrett's brandy and then
added with a chuckle, "Or midnight drink. A nightcap sounds good to me, too. You're not having anything, Lynne?"

"I already finished my...milk," Lynne lied.

"Well, isn't this cozy?" Her glance moved in a questioning way from Lynne to Jarrett. "I'm sorry if I'm intruding."

"Not at all," Jarrett said in a neutral voice.

Varina turned her back to them as she took a glass from the cupboard, and Jarrett sent Lynne a warning glance. Then he downed the rest of his brandy in a gulp and stood up.

"If you two ladies will excuse me, I'll see you both at breakfast. Lynne was just telling me that she'll be leaving in the morning." He stood up and sent Lynne an unspoken message. *Don't come to my room.* With a curt "Good night," he disappeared down the back hall.

Varina looked embarrassed. "Really, I feel terrible about this. There's no reason for you to rush off...I mean, you're perfectly welcome to stay...if you want to. Of course, I realize you came here to be alone, not share the house with me. I really apologize for the way things have turned out." Then she brightened. "If the resort gets back into operation, maybe you'd like to come back sometime for a skiing vacation?"

"Maybe," Lynne said vaguely. "Perhaps I'll change my mind and stay a few more days." She knew that Jarrett was trying to protect her, but the threatening miasma he had felt in the cellar was nothing new to her. She'd experienced it the moment she entered the house that first night. How could she leave him to the same forces that had drawn her in and out of a bewildering maelstrom?

Lynne cleared her voice. "I've found the Mitchell house very...interesting, Varina. Quite different from my modern condo. There's a richness about these old homes that's fascinating, don't you agree?"

Varina sipped her brandy. "What do you mean?"

"They carry the past with them. Don't you feel the presence of lingering spirits sometimes?"

"You mean ghosts?" Varina asked with a deprecating laugh. "Heavens no. That's a bunch of Halloween folderol."

"You don't believe that spirits linger? As if they are making a bridge between now and what has gone before?"

"What nonsense!" She shook her head, genuine amusement in her eyes. "There's no such thing as haunted houses, my dear. Just somebody's imagination working overtime."

"You've never heard or felt anything strange all the time you've lived in the house by yourself?"

Her eyes widened with mirth. "You mean spooks? Heavens no. You don't mean to tell me that you have? Pray tell, what kind of ghosts have been wandering through my house, rattling chains and flying through the air? Honey, I thought you let that good-looking Jarrett move in here with you because you were lonely—not because you were afraid of the boogeyman. Maybe it's a good thing I came back. I don't think you would have lasted a month."

"Maybe not," Lynne granted evenly.

"Some people aren't cut out to live in a place like this." Varina launched into a rambling tale about her positive reaction to the house the first time she saw it. "Everyone thought Ben married me because he needed a young housekeeper. Well, maybe he did, but we got along fine. And I was glad to have a ready-made family. I liked his son, Dave. Ben was a kind and gentle man ... a good husband." She poured another shot of brandy. Her mirth was gone.

"Griff was in love with you, too, wasn't he?"

Varina gave Lynne a guarded look as if trying to decide whether or not to tell her the truth. Then she nodded. "How did you know?"

"Just an impression he gave me. The way he was looking at you in a couple of your wedding photographs."

"My what? You've been going through my private things? I thought I had everything locked up. Out of the reach of snooping noses."

Lynne didn't want to tell her that Jarrett was the one who had found the box of photos—not in the desk drawer, as he'd said, but probably in the attic. "I'm sorry, Varina. I didn't know you would mind my looking at them. My curiosity about the family is probably out of line. Family history is always fascinating and the Mitchells certainly have had their share of drama." She knew Varina wouldn't be pleased if she found out Griff had lent her newspaper accounts to read.

She shrugged. "I guess it doesn't matter much. Griff's been sweet on me ever since we were kids. My folks had a ranch in the next valley and I was bused to school in Wolverton. We dated pretty heavy in high school and I think he was ready to marry me and settle down in Wolverton. I might have said yes if Ben hadn't come along." Her hands tightened on her glass. "Ben and I had great plans...but he died before he saw Conifer Ridge Ski Resort become a reality. And when it went bankrupt, I was glad he wasn't around to see it fail." The way her head slowly lowered, Lynne could tell that the liquor was having a depressing effect on her.

When Varina reached for the brandy a third time, Lynne stood up and said good-night. She went upstairs to her own bed and thrashed about fitfully before she finally fell asleep about three o'clock.

The sound of Jarrett's car leaving woke her the next morning. The house was cold and clammy the way it had been when she'd arrived. She jerked up and hurried to the window just in time to see his car disappear around a sharp curve. Where was he going? Had he decided to go back to Denver? Santa Fe?

She threw on her clothes and raced downstairs, intent on finding out from Varina where he'd gone. The smell of coffee greeted her when she entered the kitchen; a piece of cold toast remained on a plate. Nothing else. No sign of Varina. She must still be asleep, Lynne thought, cursing herself for not getting up early enough to slip down to Jarrett's room before he left. They had to talk!

With a nagging uneasiness, she went down the hall to his bedroom. His things were still there. The bed was unmade. His bag had been unpacked. That meant he was staying. *And so am I.*

Varina didn't get up until almost noon. The way the woman carefully moved her head told Lynne she was suffering a hangover. In contrast to her loquacious ramblings of the night before, Varina hardly said two words. Holding her head with a cupped hand as her elbow rested on the table, Varina nursed a cup of black coffee and winced when the telephone rang, but waved her hand at Lynne and said, "I'll get it."

A few minutes later as Lynne passed the library door on her way upstairs, she heard Varina snap, "Don't threaten me, Griff." The temptation to stop in the hall and eavesdrop was strong, but while Lynne hesitated, fighting with her conscience, Varina hung up. There was something going on between the two of them—but what?

Lynne spent the rest of the morning in her room, changing her sheets and doing some mending. Her senses were alert to any hint of a car coming up the slope toward the house. Drawing a chair close to the window, she made a pretense of reading. When she finally heard the roar of Jarrett's car braking in front of the house, she threw down her book. Giving her hair a quick touch and smoothing her brown sweater down over her slacks, she bounded down the stairs, expecting to see Jarrett coming into the front hall.

She paused when she reached the bottom step. He still hadn't opened the door. Puzzled, she walked across the foyer and peeked out one of the side windows. His car was there but she didn't see him. She opened the door and stepped out on the porch, blinking against the bright sunlight. When she reached the bottom step, she saw him hiking away from the house up a nearby slope. His head was bent and his arms were swinging at his side as if he were bent on covering the ground as swiftly as the five or six inches of snow would permit.

She turned and raced back upstairs, threw on her heavy jacket and a woolen scarf for her head, then dashed out the front door. A blast of lucent light like a wall stopped her before she could descend the porch steps. She threw up her hands across her face as wild spots of color whirled in front of her. When she lowered them, she was no longer alone.

A snowman grinned at her just beyond the front steps. A little boy with his back to her shoved a pipe into the mouth made of pieces of black coal. As the child stepped back, he clapped his hands and then began to skip around the snowman until he lost his balance and plopped down on his round behind. Laughing, he began tossing snow in Lynne's direction, clouding her vision. She wiped away the snow on her face, and when she lowered her hands the boy was gone and a different snowman stood there.

Two children, a boy and a girl, about the same age as the ghostly Benny, were scamping about, patting more snow on the fat tummy of a rounder snowman. Both of the children had dark hair and dark blue eyes. Then she saw Jarrett standing behind the snowman putting a stocking cap on its head. He looked at her, laughed, and then picked up a snowball and threw it at her. She raised her hands in front of her face to ward off the ball that never came. And when she lowered her hands and opened her eyes the scene was gone. Only smooth untouched snow gleamed back at her.

She walked slowly down the porch steps. Her mind wrestled with the shifting scenes that had just taken place before her eyes. Little Benny and his snowman were of the past, she knew that. Watching the child play in the snow had been no different than watching him toss his teddy bear in the air.

And what about her memories of Jarrett? How was it possible for her to remember things that had never happened— Suddenly her mouth went dry and she was filled with an insight that sent her head reeling. From the shadowed depths of her consciousness, a quiver of understanding began to stir. *They weren't memories at all.* The future had come to her as a memory. A shifting time dimension had swung her from the present into the past, into the future, and back into the present again. There was no other explanation.

The little boy had played in the snowy front yard almost thirty years in the past. The two children she would bear would build their own snowman in the same spot in the future. She had already seen their nursery and heard their cries. She thought back over all the memories that had come to her about Jarrett. They had been real—only they hadn't happened *yet.* A bubbling joy swept through her.

Filled with a sense of impending discovery, she headed in the direction Jarrett had gone, thankful that his boots had made a clear path in the snow. Excitement began to build. A hot sweat enveloped her body. Even though her breath was shallow in the chilled air, she bent her head and trudged up the hillside as if each moment lost were a whip at her back.

When she reached the ridge she'd followed on her first outing, she realized that Jarrett was heading in the same direction she had taken that day—toward the crosses. When the high bluff came into view, she could see his distant figure standing in front of the rock memorial.

Her memory delivered a vision of him standing there holding the hands of two children—their own little boy and girl twins. With a burst of joy, Lynne now knew with certainty that all the memories she had of this man lay ahead. In a bewildering time warp, the future had been given to her as a memory. And the dead little boy was somehow linked to their happy future.

She waved to Jarrett but he didn't see her. He was looking down at something in his hand. When she reached him, he didn't look at her or say anything; he just held it out to her, his dark eyes shadowed with confusion. In the middle of his palm lay a small red block.

CHAPTER SIXTEEN

For a moment Lynne just stared at the block as a rush of emotion overtook her. She had forgotten all about it and couldn't remember what she'd done with it. There was no doubt in her mind that it was the same one she'd found lying on the floor that first morning. She remembered that she had picked up the block later and held it in her hand the way Jarrett was doing. The present had slipped into the past that time, and she'd watched the little boy playing with his teddy bear, but the happy moment had dissolved in terror. The remembrance of the fear in his face brought a shiver down her back. The way Jarrett was staring at the block, she knew he was experiencing the same kind of bewildering sensation she had felt when it nestled in her hand.

"Where did you get it?" She searched his shadowed expression.

"I found it at the bottom of the cellar steps last night," he said slowly. "At first I didn't know what it was, but when I picked it up I felt a rush of emotions that left me stunned." He swallowed hard. "Once I had it in my hand it was like all the fear I'd ever felt in my whole life rushed at me."

"Why didn't you say something last night? Why didn't you tell me?"

He took a deep breath. "Tell you what? That a child's block was scaring the hell out of me?"

"It's Benny's," Lynne said, turning around and pointing to the cross that bore the child's name. "It's his block."

Jarrett stared at her. He had trouble working his mouth and his voice was scratchy as he asked, "How do you know?"

"I saw him playing with it." Lynne's tone was matter-of-fact. "On the living room rug—but it was green. Back in the sixties the room was furnished in shades of green."

"Do you know what you're saying?" He looked at the cross and then back at her. "You dreamed that you saw the dead child playing with blocks?" The edge of disbelief in his voice was sharp and unmistakable.

"I've seen Benny lots of times," she responded evenly. "Just now he was making a snowman in front of the house."

"Good heavens, Lynne. Do you know what you're saying? You're talking about a kid who has been dead for over twenty-five years."

"I know." Lynne pointed at the names imprinted on the bronze marker. "I've seen them all. In fact, I've been with them—in the past."

"What?"

"The first night in the house, they woke me up. I heard laughter and music and when I came down to the living room they were all there." She pointed to the names on two of the crosses. "Maribelle and Sue Ann Ashley. Pretty girls, both had long dark hair. They were laughing and talking together on the sofa. Benjamin Mitchell stood in front of the fireplace, smiling at them. He had peppered gray hair and a well-conditioned body that radiated energy and good health. Little Benny was playing on the floor, as I said." She smiled reassuringly at Jarrett. She could tell he was having trouble accepting what she was saying. "The next morning, I couldn't remember anything about it. Even when I found the red block, my mind wouldn't give up any memory of the experience—not until I came up here and saw the memorial. Then the past came rushing aback and I knew that I had been slipped back in time."

He swallowed hard. "It's too... bizarre."

"I know. I didn't understand it at first myself. But it's happened more than once. You have to believe me, sometimes the past becomes the present. The furnishings in the house change and I live a scene that took place more than twenty-five years ago. Ever since I arrived, I've been plunged back and forth—and even ahead—in time."

"How can you be so... so damn calm? This is crazy. I don't believe this kind of thing happens in real life."

"What is real?" she asked quietly.

"This moment... us... now... in the present."

"And all the moments in the future?"

"What?"

She smiled. He wasn't ready to be hit with the future as she'd already experienced it. If fate was kind, he would be a part of it. "If time is like a revolving belt, maybe the human spirit can get off and on at different places, sometimes in the past, sometimes in the present . . . and sometimes in the future."

"That's crazy."

"I know." She studied Jarrett's face . . . the firm lines of his chin, the arched eyebrows over his indigo eyes and the smooth lines of his nose. "There's one thing I haven't figured out. The photograph I found on your dresser—the one with your name on the back?"

He was startled. "You know about that?"

"There's an undeniable resemblance to pictures of Benny. I think it's time you started leveling with me."

He took her arm and they began hiking back along the high ridge toward the house. "My story's going to sound as unbelievable as yours. When I first saw an old brochure about Conifer Ridge Ski Resort and the surrounding area, I was struck by a startling sense of déjà vu. There was no logical reason that I should feel drawn to the place—I'd never been in this part of Colorado. Until I was approached by an investor to look into the defunct resort as a financial investment, I'd never had any intention of coming here." He shrugged. "I can't explain it, but the scenes in the brochure of the valley and Wolverton were like a forgotten dream, and when I got here and saw the Sawtooth Mountains and the Mitchell house, the feeling of recognition intensified." He gave her a wry smile. "Remember how familiar I seemed to be with the house that first day?"

"Yes, I remember. And I suspected that you'd stretched the truth a bit just so you could stay in the house. But why? What were you looking for?"

"My past."

She stopped and caught his arm. "Your past? But you told me that you were born and raised in Santa Fe?"

"Raised . . . not born. I'm adopted. I didn't find out until a few years ago—not that it mattered. I have the most wonderful parents in the world. It wasn't being adopted that bothered me." There was a hard set to his mouth. She didn't understand the bitterness that flashed into his eyes. "What is it?" she asked.

"I've had a hard time accepting the fact that I had been tossed away like an unwanted piece of garbage. My foster parents told me that I had been found abandoned by the side of the road. No one knew how old I was. They guessed at my age . . . two or three. I was nearly dead when they found me and was slow in getting back my speech."

"I'm so sorry." She touched his cheek. "I've worked with abandoned children. I know how traumatic such a revelation must have been for you."

The muscles in his cheek flickered. He slipped his arm around her waist and they began hiking over the rough terrain again. Their footsteps crackled in the crisp snow.

"But I still don't understand. Why would you have memories of the Mitchell house?"

He shook his head. "I don't know."

"And why would you resemble Benny—unless you were related?" Her eyes widened. "Could you be a brother or a cousin?"

"I suppose I could be." He sighed. "None of it makes sense. Why would a piece of wood trigger all kinds of feelings inside me? I couldn't sleep last night and this morning I drove to Wolverton. I decided that since Griff's been a longtime friend of the Mitchell family, he might know things that nobody else did."

"And did you get some information from him?"

"No. Actually, he acted as if I'd lost my mind when I told him I thought I might have some ties to the Mitchell family. He didn't seem to have any interest in me or my story."

"He was lying. Griff took your picture and one of Benny that I showed him. I put the photos on the counter, and when I looked for them after he left, they were gone. Why would he take them?"

"He didn't say anything about them!" said Jarrett angrily. "All the time, he had my picture. I intended to show it around as soon as the time seemed right."

She caught her breath. "Do you think…no, it's too crazy."

"Go ahead, tell me. At this point nothing is too crazy."

Lynne moistened her lips. "Because Griff is acting so funny, I wondered if he might know who your biological parents are."

Jarrett walked in silence, staring ahead, squinting against the bright sun. Lynne glanced at his rigid profile, her mind whirling in all directions.

"Maybe Benjamin or his son, Dave, had an illegitimate child," she speculated. "Griff could have known about it... maybe even been involved."

"I don't see how."

"Neither do I, but I sense that Varina's half-frightened of him. I heard her talking to him this morning and she said, 'Don't threaten me, Griff.'"

"He probably called her after I left his office."

"Why would he be threatening her?"

"I don't know." He tightened the arm around her waist. "But I don't want you to stay here. Let me handle things. When I start demanding some answers, there's no telling what will happen. Both of us have experienced an insidious danger that could erupt at any moment."

"I'm not leaving."

"You don't need to get involved."

"Involved?" She laughed up at him. "Too late, Jarrett. From the moment I saw a picture of the house, I accepted the truth that I had no choice but to come here and see what fate had in store for me." She sobered. "And I did try to leave, but the spirits of Benny and his grandfather wouldn't let me."

"How can you say that?"

"Because it's true. I have to stay until..."

"Until what?"

She couldn't answer. For a long moment, they looked down the sloping hillside from the high ridge. The mountain scene was one of hushed tranquility. All ugliness was covered in a mantle of snow. The house and the snow-covered remains of the resort nestled cozily at the base of the mountain. A wispy wreath of smoke rose in lazy spirals from one of the chimneys of the house.

"We'll find the answers," she said with confidence.

"I've never believed in fate before." He turned around and pulled her close against his body. "But I accept without reservation any mysterious plan that has brought you to me."

Warm clouds of breath mingled as he tenderly and possessively laid his mouth on hers. The scarf slipped off her head, allowing the sun to touch her hair and bring a lovely glint of copper to the tousled strands. "Beautiful," he murmured.

The wild singing of her own heart welcomed the hand he slipped inside her jacket to find the rounded softness of her breast. His fingers caressed her with the same persuasive rhythm of his kiss, firing every sense until she groaned in protest.

As they embraced on the snow-covered mountain, the blue sky arching above them, he murmured her name over and over again. His whispers were a beloved incantation bonding her to him in a mystical litany. For a brief moment they stayed suspended in time, the happiness found in each other's arms the only reality.

Reluctantly Jarrett pulled away, and the world rushed back. He held Lynne's hand firmly in his as they descended the high ridge to the valley below—where the house waited.

CHAPTER SEVENTEEN

They entered the house through the back door. Varina wasn't in the kitchen, but an opened can of soup and dirty bowl indicated that she had already eaten lunch. No sign of her on the ground floor. Lynne slipped upstairs and saw that the woman's bedroom door was closed. Probably sleeping off her hangover, Lynne thought. She returned to the kitchen with a light step. It was almost like having the house to themselves again.

Jarrett was putting together some ham-and-cheese sandwiches. The morning's exercise had made them both hungry and they moved about the kitchen in pleasant harmony as they set lunch out on the table. *Just like always,* she thought, accepting the memories that filled her mind.

As she passed him, heading toward the refrigerator for beer, he playfully blocked her way. "Toll charge." He leaned toward her for a kiss, holding a mustard-covered knife in one hand and a piece of bread in the other.

"And if I refuse to pay?" she teased. The playful ritual was familiar...sometimes it was jelly, sometimes butter or something else. *He's going to put mustard on the tip of my nose.*

He swiped her nose lightly with the knife. "There. That's what happens when you don't pay up."

She laughed. "Yes, I know." And she kissed him Eskimo-style, putting the smudge of yellow mustard on his nose. She laughed and slipped away before he could retaliate.

Although they kept the conversation light through lunch, Lynne could tell that Jarrett's thoughts were heavier than his banter indicated. He's having trouble handling everything I told him this morning, she thought. And no wonder! Who would readily believe that she had traveled back in time . . . or forward? And the puzzle of his own connection to the Mitchell family must be eating away at him.

As if reading her thoughts, he took out the child's block from his pocket and looked at it. Then he handed it to her with a challenge in his eyes. She knew what he was saying. *Show me.*

She hesitated. There were too many forces at work, too many incomprehensible tangles. She was fearful of tempting any fate that might snatch Jarrett from her. All the things that had happened to her had not been of her own making. She had never courted the sliding time line that had plunged her into the past. It had just happened. She had become a medium for the spirits who had died tragically in the avalanche and been killed in the car accident. She had seen them, been with them, and had felt the child's joy and terror. What if she had unwittingly released the evil that both she and Jarrett had felt?

Reluctantly, she took the block in her hand. She waited for a moment and then smiled in relief. Nothing. The piece of wood was just that. No warmth. No projection. She even rubbed it with one of her fingers and felt the roughly painted surface. Nothing more. She looked at Jarrett and shook her head, handing the block back to him.

His fingers closed over the toy as hers had done. She watched his face. The night before, he had been caught up in a wave of explosive emotion when he picked up the block at the foot of the stairs. She could tell his body was tensed against the return of that shattering sense of evil. When his expression remained neutral, she knew the block had not delivered any disquieting sensation to him.

"This is crazy," he said, flashing an impatient look at her.

"I know, but it doesn't make it any less real," she protested.

He pushed back his chair and got up.

"Where are you going?"

"Back down to the cellar."

Her mouth was suddenly dry. She wanted to protest, persuade him to leave it alone. If his experience was anything like hers, he'd be swept up in another emotional upheaval soon enough. She was afraid. The set of his chin told her it would do no good to argue. "All right." She stood up. "I'm coming with you."

He gave her a worried look. "I don't suppose it would do any good to tell you to wait here?"

"None at all."

He started to say something more and then decided against it. He turned away. "I'll get another light bulb for the top of the stairs. No sense wandering around in the dark. I should have done it last night but my imagination was firing on all cylinders and I wasn't thinking clearly."

It wasn't your imagination. Lynne was certain his experience had been as real and valid as the ones that had shaken her.

They swiped a bulb from the reading lamp in his room, which was a lower wattage than the one they then replaced at the top of the cellar stairs, but they hadn't found any spare bulbs in the kitchen cupboards. Jarrett turned on his flashlight as they went down the stairs.

The dank fusty smell was like that of a dirt cave. A bare bulb hung on a chain from one of the wooden rafters, and when Jarrett pulled the string, a bright circle of light bathed the dirt floor. A modern furnace and hot-water heater using Butane gas stood on a small concrete slab. An old coal chute still contained a good amount of coal, and Lynne suspected that Varina used it in the fireplace sometimes instead of wood. The walls were rock and the ceiling was made of dark wooden planks.

Jarrett's head almost touched the low ceiling as he moved about the small enclosure. "Well, well. A smelly old cellar dug out of the hill to hold a furnace and not much else."

She couldn't tell if it was relief or a secret suspicion that he'd acted like a fool that was responsible for his laughter. He had been certain that the answer to his emotional trauma of the evening before would show up in concrete terms. *It doesn't work that way. The old house doesn't give up its secrets that easily.* She kept her silence and watched him.

Very deliberately he passed the flashlight over every inch of the dirt floor and rock walls, searching for anything that could account for the disquieting experience that had engulfed him the night before.

"There's nothing here."

She nodded and added silently, *Not that we can see.*

He shrugged and turned back toward the stairs. Then he stopped. His expression changed. The tight lines came back in his face, his eyes narrowed. Slowly he walked over to the space under the stairs. There was a rusty nail sticking out of a board. Jarrett reached out and pulled on it. A small door about two feet square opened, revealing a crawl space under the stairs. He flashed the light around the enclosure.

Lynne choked back a cry. Lying just inside the small space was a brown teddy bear with one ear missing. Nothing else. The cloth fell apart in Jarrett's hands as he lifted the stuffed animal, but the bear's face with its black-button eyes remained intact.

"It's Benny's," she breathed. "I've watched him play with it." The past merged with the present as she reached out and took the stuffed animal that the phantom little boy had laughingly tossed in the air. "All these years it has lain hidden under the stairs. I bet this is the reason you were drawn to the cellar. The little boy wanted you to find his toy."

Jarrett looked at her as if she were talking gibber-
ish. She smothered a rise of impatience. *He still doesn't
understand.* In spite of everything, it was obvious that
Jarrett had reservations about all that she'd told him.
Not that his disbelief was surprising. He was a busi-
nessman, dealing with empirical data. It was no wonder that his ordered mind would reject such absurd
claims that she'd slipped into the past to be with the
little boy and his teddy bear. If he hadn't been on an
emotional quest of his own, he would have undoubtedly discounted the whole thing as utter nonsense,
Lynne thought. Even now, the way he stared at the
crumpling teddy bear in her hands revealed a mind in
utter confusion, struggling to come to terms with an
impossible situation. Her impatience faded.

"Come on," she said gently. "Let's go back upstairs." He nodded, deep lines creasing his forehead.
Lynne turned toward the stairs and had mounted the
first step when she stopped abruptly and looked upward. The landing light was suddenly shut from view
by the black form of a man standing there.

For a moment she didn't know whether he was real
or a phantom. Something in the way he held himself
made her think he was going to slam the door shut on
them before they could get to the top of the stairs.

Then he spoke gruffly. "What in the hell are you two
doing down there?"

"Griff!" She let out her breath in relief. "You startled me."

Jarrett brushed past her as if he, too, had the impression that the man was about to trap them in the

cellar. His body tensed for a fight, he reached the top step. When Griff didn't move, Jarrett glared up at him, several steps lower than the landing where Griff stood towering over him. "You're in the way."

Lynne's heart began to beat rapidly. The men stood like two stags facing each other. Jarrett would have difficulty keeping his balance if Griff put those mammoth hands on him and gave him a shove backward.

At that moment, Lynne heard Varina's voice. "What's going on? Griff? I didn't hear you come in. What are you doing?" The cellar door swung open wider. Varina's head appeared as she stared at Griff and Jarrett. Then her gaze traveled down the stairs to where Lynne stood at the bottom. "For heaven's sake, what on earth are you people doing in the cellar?"

The question was a logical one. Lynne just hoped to heaven they could come up with a logical answer. She let out the breath she'd been holding as Griff left the landing. Jarrett waited on the stairs for Lynne and took her arm in a protective gesture as they went back into the kitchen.

Varina centered an astonished look on each of them in turn. Griff...Jarrett...Lynne. "Would someone please explain what is going on in *my* house...or rather in *my* cellar?"

Griff's thick eyebrows matted over his craggy nose. "I heard talking and found the two of them down there." His dark eyes were hostile. Once again Lynne wondered if he would have slammed the door shut on them if Varina hadn't intervened.

Varina's questioning eyes swung to Jarrett and Lynne. Before either of them could say anything, her gaze fell to the tattered teddy bear in Lynne's hands. "What on earth is that?" Her nose wrinkled in distaste. "Looks like something dead."

Lynne held it out for her to see. Some of the stuffing fell out on the floor and dust rose from the places where Lynne held the decaying cloth.

"I still don't know what it is," said Varina impatiently.

"A teddy bear."

"A what?" Varina looked more perplexed than ever.

"A teddy bear. A stuffed toy. It belonged to Benny Mitchell," Lynne said boldly.

Varina stared at the old toy and then her eyes widened. "Little Benny? Yes...yes...I remember now. He loved that bear." She turned to Griff. "Don't you remember how he always carried it around? But how did it get down in the cellar? I thought he had it with him the day of the avalanche." She frowned. "It's been so long." Varina sat down at the table as if caught up in a surge of memories.

Lynne tried to read Varina's thoughts but couldn't. The teddy bear had obviously been a cue for dredging up the forgotten past. Not knowing what to do with the old toy, Lynne found a paper sack and put the bear inside. She couldn't throw it away, maybe because it validated the time-warp contact she'd had with the little boy.

Jarrett seemed to collect himself under Varina's scrutiny. He gave her that people-management smile of his and walked over to the refrigerator. "How about a beer, Griff?" he asked pleasantly as if he were the host of the house.

Lynne was glad to have him take charge of the situation. She watched him as he handed the burly man a can of beer. He said casually, "Lynne tells me you took a couple of old photographs that she showed you the other day."

Instead of denying it, Griff nodded. He took a swig of beer and then wiped his mouth. "Yep."

"Why didn't you say something about them this morning?"

Griff leveled steady eyes at Jarrett. "Cause I'm trying to figure out what you're up to."

Varina's head jerked up as if she'd been tuned out to the conversation until that point. Annoyance was written all over her face as she glared up at Griff. "What on earth are you talking about, Griff? Everyone knows what Jarrett's doing here."

"Do we?" he said in a sarcastic tone.

Varina's eyes snapped. "I've had just about enough of your interference, Griff. I've put up with it all these years out of friendship, but enough's enough. I'll thank you kindly to keep your nose out of my business . . . beginning right now!"

Griff slammed down the can of beer on the table. "You've got it, lady. But don't say I didn't warn you." He stalked out of the room and the front door slammed behind him.

"That man," Varina breathed angrily. "You'd think he'd get the message after all these years that I'm not

interested in him . . . never have been . . . never will be.''
She walked over to a cupboard and took out the brandy
bottle. ''I didn't even know he was here. He wanders
in and out like he owns the place.'' She poured a generous amount of brandy in a glass. Then she turned to
Jarrett. ''What do you say we go over those state-
ments again? I'd like to show you the profit sheets on
the lodge and the ski rentals.''

''Good idea,'' Jarrett said with an enthusiasm that
left Lynne feeling cold. How could he think about
business when there were so many unanswered questions in his own life? The man she loved seemed able to
compartmentalize his thoughts and emotions with an-
noying efficiency. Lynne wanted to talk out her feelings but instead she vented her frustrations by cleaning
up the kitchen mess.

When she'd finished she went into Jarrett's room
and lay down on his bed. She didn't care what Varina
thought.

Nearly two hours passed before he opened the door
to his bedroom. His face flickered with surprise when
he saw her and then his forehead creased with worry
lines. He sat down on the edge of the bed and took her
hands. ''I think you should leave...tomorrow. I'm not
comfortable in this situation...with all the unanswered questions.''

''Then maybe *we* ought to leave.'' He avoided her
eyes as she looked up at him. She wished that he would
lay down beside her.

"No. I can't. For one thing I have to finish my work. But there's no reason for you to stay."

"I can think of one," she responded softly. Why didn't he look at her? "I don't want to leave you."

He sighed. "I've had a lot of questions eating at me for a long time. The most important thing at the moment is for me to find some answers." He looked at her then, his dark eyes full of pain. "How can I think about a family of my own, children, when I don't even know what kind of a heredity I'm passing along? The truth is that someone gave me birth and then threw me away."

She saw the anguish in his face and she pulled him down beside her. There were no answers she could give him, but she refused to let him shut her out. She had seen too many abandoned children suffering from the same kind of torturing uncertainty.

She massaged his neck and pressed her lips to his with gentle persuasion.

She felt the tension ease from his body and they made love as if the wonderment of having found each other was the only reality that was firm and unchanging.

Later, she lay quietly in his arms, content until she entertained a thought that sent a quiver of apprehension through her. What if he discovered something about himself that changed everything between them? Maybe he didn't really belong to her after all?

CHAPTER EIGHTEEN

With most of the afternoon gone, they slipped back into the kitchen like conspirators and found it empty. They took a peek in the library. No Varina. She must have retired to her room, Lynne thought.

"Well, my lady, what's on the menu for dinner?" Jarrett asked as they returned to the kitchen.

She slid her arms around his waist. "Didn't you say we had some steaks?"

He slipped his lips down to the soft curve of her neck and nibbled. "Hmm. Delicious."

She giggled and moved away. "I'm serious."

"So am I." He reached for her but she evaded his clutches.

"Here, Chef. You do the steaks." She thrust a white package from the meat tray into his hands.

"Me?" He pretended to be unwilling but she knew that he always prided himself on doing steaks exactly right. He'd broil them until they were a delicate pink, juicy and tender. She leaned up against the counter smiling at him.

"Let's eat in the dining room again," he suggested as she started to prepare a salad.

"What about Varina?"

"We'll surprise her," he said with a grin.

"She might not like the idea of us using her linens and china."

He grinned. "So let her kick us out. We'll be leaving tomorrow anyway."

"We will?" She looked puzzled. Earlier he had insisted that she go while he stayed.

"Yes, I've decided I'll take you to meet my folks in Santa Fe. We'll get an early start first thing in the morning." His voice was gentle and reassuring. "I'm sure we'll both get a different perspective on things once we're away from the house. My parents will love you and you'll be delighted with New Mexico's land of enchantment."

As he talked about his home state, a nagging puzzlement spoiled Lynne's complete bliss. Why had he changed his mind all of a sudden? Why was he content to leave unanswered all the questions that had been plaguing him? She had watched him tenaciously dig for every fact to make his financial report complete. Simply to leave the mountains of Colorado behind and ignore the unsettling feelings that had brought him to the area was out of character.

He's coming back.

He intended to get her out of the way and then return. Did he think she was too stupid to see through his duplicity? Sudden impatience fueled every snap of the knife as she cut up carrots and celery for a salad.

"Wow! You must really hate vegetables," he teased.

"No, I hate being manipulated." Her eyes blazed as she swung on him.

"Now, what does that mean?"

"You weren't successful in getting me out of the house on my own, so now you are going to personally accompany my departure."

"Don't you want to go to Santa Fe with me?"

"That's not the point, and you know it! Don't play me for a fool, Jarrett."

"And don't you be a stubborn mule. I don't know what in the hell is going on, but I want you out of it."

They glared at each other. Lynne's hands were clenched and Jarrett's chin was stiff and unyielding. At that moment Varina's footsteps sounded in the hall.

"My goodness, what's going on here? Dinner underway already?" she asked as she came into the kitchen. "I didn't hear you come downstairs, Lynne. I thought you were still napping in your room?" There was a questioning lilt in her tone.

Lynne mumbled something vague.

"Did you have a good rest, Varina?" Jarrett asked smoothly.

"Wonderful." Varina laughed. "It's really great to be back in this mountain air. I don't know how you can stand Chicago year-round, Lynne. As the old saying goes, a city is a great place to visit but nobody should have to live there."

"I rather like the noise and bustle," Lynne answered, knowing she was being arbitrary.

Varina looked at Jarrett tending the steaks and Lynne adding cream of mushroom soup to a can of French green beans. "Is there something I can do? Gracious sakes, I feel like a guest in my own house."

"We thought we'd eat in the dining room, Varina...kind of a farewell celebration," Jarrett said, "since Lynne and I will be leaving in the morning."

Lynne clamped her mouth shut and didn't say anything.

"In the morning," Varina echoed, her expression suddenly crestfallen. "You're both welcome to stay longer, you know. I don't mind at all. Love the company. And maybe I could be of further help in your report, Jarrett?" she offered hopefully.

"Thanks, I think I have everything I need. If anything unexpected arises, I can come back."

And won't that be a surprise? Lynne thought sarcastically. Aloud she said, "I'll set the table."

Lynne silently fumed all through dinner, irritated with Varina's monologues and Jarrett's unruffled good manners.

Finally, when she couldn't stand it any longer, she put down her fork and turned toward him. "Jarrett, didn't you have some personal questions to ask Varina about the Mitchell family? I mean, since we're leaving tomorrow and won't be back anytime soon..." Lynne let a pause punctuate the remark. "Now's a good time, don't you think?"

Varina looked puzzled. "What kind of personal questions?"

Jarrett's glare would have chilled an arctic glacier but Lynne only smiled back at him. She turned to Varina and plunged ahead. "Jarrett was adopted and he's interested in finding his natural parents. We think they may have been related to the Mitchell family in some way."

"Really?" She turned rounded eyes on Jarrett. "I don't understand."

Jarrett leaned back in his chair. With obvious emotion, he told Varina about his childhood abandonment. "Lately, the need to find my roots has become kind of an obsession. Anyway, when I saw pictures of this area, the mountains and the house seemed familiar to me. Probably wishful thinking on my part," he admitted.

"And maybe not," Lynne said firmly. "There's a decided family resemblance."

"But how could that be? Heaven's sake, what a mystery!" Excitement glinted in Varina's eyes. "I really don't know everything about Ben's family. I think he had a cousin living in Colorado Springs for a while. They had a parcel of kids. Donald Mitchell...that was his name. I guess Donald would be about the right age to be your dad. I know that he had a bunch of kids and they used to spend some lengthy visits with Benjamin. I never did cotton to him or his wife. Frankly, I wouldn't be surprised if they abandoned more than one of their kids." Her eyes darkened. "Wouldn't that be something? I think he moved back to Texas. Let me go see if I can find his address." She stood up and left the table.

Lynne cast a furtive glance at Jarrett, relieved to see that his expression had softened. Forcing the conversation had been an impulsive, reckless act, but she was glad that they'd gleaned valuable information. Tracking down the members of the Mitchell family might provide some interesting answers...and perhaps some frightening ones, as well.

She covered Jarrett's hand with her own. "I know you didn't want to pursue any of this until I was safely away in Santa Fe, but wherever the trail leads, I want to be there."

He gave her an exasperated look. "I should have known you wouldn't behave yourself and do what I wanted." He sighed and then leaned over and gave her a quick kiss. "You don't have to be so concerned about me," he chided.

You're my future, she answered silently. *And I have to take care of it.*

Varina came back with the address written on a slip of paper. "I'm not sure it's a current one. I haven't had much contact with them through the years. I think they resented me from the beginning."

"Thanks for your help." Jarrett smiled at her and put the slip of paper in his pocket.

"How about coffee in the living room?" suggested Varina. "I think I can find some family albums from Benjamin's side of the family that you might want to look at. Just leave the cleanup," she ordered as Lynne stood up. "You both fixed the meal, I'll do the wash-up later."

Varina led the way down the hall to the front room. Lynne would have preferred to sit in the library. The living room held too many cues for remembering the bizarre experiences she'd had as she moved in and out of the present. She was tense just sitting on the couch while Jarrett and Varina took chairs beside a coffee table. Varina collected some old leather-covered albums for them to look at. As Lynne sipped her coffee, she began to relax. A drowsy feeling eased up into her arms and legs.

Varina was talking excitedly, pointing out people to Jarrett. Their voices faded away and Lynne's head suddenly dropped back on the sofa. She willed her heavy eyes to stay open even as they closed.

When her eyelids slowly lifted, she knew on some detached level that she had slipped into the past again. She was no longer looking at the ceiling of the living room. Above her a clear blue sky was dotted with vaporous white clouds. The air was brisk upon her face as she trudged up a snowy mountainside. And she wasn't alone.

"Faster, Grandpa, faster," squealed the little boy.

Lynne turned around. Benny was sitting in a sled pulled by the gray-haired Benjamin, who was wearing snowshoes. Lynne looked behind them and saw two young women poling through the snow on cross-country skis.

The day was bright, the mountainside hushed and tranquil. Smooth banks of deep snow swept upward to vistas of frosted trees and crystal peaks. The scene was one of utter tranquillity—until a sharp report of a gun sliced harshly through the air. A rippling of vibrations sounded high upon a nearby slope and was followed by an ominous rumbling. Masses of snow trembled. Like the walls of a giant fortress collapsing, the hillside began to slide downward, moving faster and faster, louder and louder.

"Avalanche!" Benjamin shouted, and waved at the two women to turn back. He jerked around and grabbed the sled. With a violent shove, he sent it sailing toward a ravine that sloped away from the descending mass of rocks and snow. Lynne felt the billowy snow on her face, watched in horror as mammoth waves of snow swept downward, rising and falling. She cried out in a soundless scream as she watched Benjamin and the two pretty sisters disappear under tons of rock, trees and snow.

A movement far below brought Lynne's eyes down to the ravine, where a woman with a shotgun stood. She watched as the boy's sled careered to safety before it turned over and spilled the child out on the ground.

"Benny! Benny!" The name was a croaking sob. Lynne tried to move toward the woman and the child, but they faded from view.

Lynne's eyes fluttered open. The past was gone. But not the horror. The vicious assault on her body was the same one she'd experienced before—only this time it was in the present.

Varina stood over her. "You meddling fool!" The woman struck Lynne's face with clawed hands that scratched her cheeks. She grabbed a fistful of Lynne's blouse and began ripping. "A lovers' quarrel, that's what it will look like."

Lynne struggled to protect herself from the onslaught but her arms were too heavy. *Drugged. The coffee!* Jarrett's head lolled to one side as he slumped in his chair. "Jarrett! Jarrett!"

"He can't help you," Varina snarled, standing over Lynne and pointing a black revolver at her. "Your sweetheart shoots you and then himself. His nine lives are over." She sent him a look of raw hate. "It was a fluke that he escaped being buried with the others. I should have made certain the brat was dead before I dumped him in New Mexico. At the time I thought it was better not to kill him because it seemed unlikely anyone would connect a live child with one supposed dead. And everyone knew Benny was dead. Dead. Dead." Varina's voice rose to a frenzied pitch. "The property was mine. Mine. Mine. I couldn't let him take it from me. Not then . . . not now!"

Lynne tried to work her thick tongue. "Don't . . . don't do this. . . ."

"I messed up once. I won't foul up a second time." Jarrett had begun to move slightly in his chair. Maybe he was fighting off the drugged coffee, Lynne hoped. If she could keep Varina's attention on her, maybe Jarrett could do something before the woman shot them both.

"You can't . . . get away . . . with it. Not . . . a second time." Lynne's words were slow and labored. Her head whirled dizzily and she knew that she was in danger of passing out any second.

Varina laughed. "Of course I can. I'm a respected widow—they'll believe me."

"Griff won't," Lynne mumbled with sudden insight. "He knows . . . doesn't he?" She swallowed to put some moisture in her mouth. "He knows...you caused the avalanche?"

Varina's eyes flashed. "He doesn't have any proof. Besides—" her mouth twisted in an ugly smile "—he loves me...always has. He'll do anything I say."

"How...how can you...be sure?" Out of the corner of her eye, Lynne saw that Jarrett was sitting up.

Varina saw him, too, and jerked around. She raised the gun in her hand. "Time to go back to being a ghost, Benny Mitchell."

"No," Lynne cried. She gave a drunken lunge off the couch and managed to get her arms around Varina's waist. She locked her grip as best she could, holding on as Varina tried to move away.

"Let go!"

Lynne stuck out her legs in a clumsy gesture and her dead weight put Varina off balance. She stumbled and fell to her knees. As Varina tried to right herself, Lynne knocked the gun from her hand.

The weapon slid across the floor, close to where Jarrett was sitting. He staggered upward out of his chair, but in his drugged state his legs wouldn't hold him. They gave way and he crumpled heavily to the floor, striking his head on the corner of the coffee table.

With a wild shriek, Varina scrambled toward the gun. Lynne tightened, her scissorslike grip around Varina's waist trying to hold her back. Varina struck her in the face and Lynne's grasp began to weaken. She couldn't hold on. Her drugged state was no match for the crazed woman's fury.

Varina got away and grabbed the gun. With a triumphant cry, she lurched to her feet. Jarrett made a guttural protest and Varina swung around, the gun in her hand ready to fire at him.

Terror leapt into the woman's face. She took a couple of staggering steps backward. Lynne raised her head and followed Varina's shocked gaze.

In a protective stance in front of Jarrett's slumped body stood a transparent specter—Benjamin Mitchell. Jarrett's grandfather.

The ghostly figure began moving toward Varina.

She raised her gun and fired, pulling the trigger again and again. The bullets bit harmlessly into the far wall. The apparition of her dead husband kept coming.

With a wild cry, she dropped the empty gun and fled out of the house with the ghost floating after her.

Lynne lurched to Jarrett's side. His head wobbled the same way that she'd seen Dave Mitchell's head slump forward when he was driving the car that went over the cliff. She knew then that Ben's son had not been drunk. He must have been drugged by Varina. Tears filled Lynne's eyes, thinking of the two innocent young people who had been the first victims of Varina's greed.

The ghost of Benjamin Mitchell must have been riding with Varina as she drove away from the house in her cream-colored Subaru. She didn't make it around the first curve. Lynne heard the crunch of metal and glass as the car went over the sheer precipice just below the house. And then there was silence.

Jarrett looked at Lynne with glazed eyes. "What...happened?"

She pushed back the thick shock of black hair. Her throat was parched but her smile was steady. "Your grandfather just saved your life a second time."

CHAPTER NINETEEN

It was an hour and a half before Sheriff McDermit responded to Jarrett's 911 call. By that time Lynne and Jarrett had drunk numerous cups of black coffee and had repeatedly walked up and down the hall, holding on to each other as they fought the drug that had raced through their system.

The sheriff was a lanky fellow in his thirties who wore a heavy plaid jacket, a cowboy hat and pants stuffed in a pair of alligator boots. His ruddy complexion matched his sandy hair, and clear blue eyes reflected a calm, intelligent handling of his job. Griff was with him and the editor's slumped shoulders and distraught expression were a sharp contrast to the officer's.

"Varina..." he choked, running an agitated hand through his bushy beard.

He didn't need to finish. There was no doubt in Lynne's mind that the ghost of Benjamin had ridden with her over the side of the sheer mountain cliff. His son's death had been avenged.

Jarrett pointed out the black revolver that Varina had dropped on her way out of the house and the bullet holes in the living room wall. Lynne left Jarrett to answer the questions and she went into the library and waited for the three men to join her. She now had most of the answers from that last sojourn into the past and from what Varina had revealed in her anger. She expected Griff to be able to fill in the rest.

She was glad when he came in alone, leaving the sheriff and Jarrett still talking in the front room. He sat down wearily in a chair and rested his head in his hands.

Lynne said softly, "You knew that the avalanche was caused by a shot Varina fired into the mountain snow mass, didn't you?"

He raised pain-filled eyes. "I didn't know for sure...but I suspected it. While the rescue team was poling for the victims that day, I came back to the house. Quite by accident, I found one of Ben's rifles out of place in the game room and the barrel was slightly warm. I couldn't figure it out because Varina was in Denver...or supposed to be." He shook his head. "I knew how badly she wanted plans for the new Conifer Ridge Ski Resort to go forward and she couldn't stand it when Ben changed his mind about the whole thing. He decided that the commercial venture would ruin everything he loved about this place so he backed out."

"So she killed him...and two other innocent people. And Dave and Carole before that. I'm sure she drugged them so Dave would lose control of the car. And when little Benny survived the avalanche she had to get rid of him, too."

He nodded. "Ben hadn't changed his will when he married, so everything went to his grandson. I heard

Jarrett tell his story to the sheriff just now. I can see how *disappointed* Varina must have been when by some miracle the boy escaped the fate of the others.''

Not a miracle, Lynne corrected silently. *The love of a grandfather saved him.* Griff would never believe that she had relived that moment of tragedy with the victims. Aloud, she said, ''Varina had to get rid of Benny in some other way...without raising any suspicions.''

He sighed. ''Who would connect an abandoned three-year-old in New Mexico with a boy believed to have been killed in a Colorado avalanche?''

''How could she do that to an innocent child?''

''She never liked Benny. She was jealous of the way Ben doted on him. She told me once she used to shut him up in the cellar.''

That's why Jarrett felt such terror down there. His subconscious remembered.

''And you didn't say anything to Ben?'' she flared angrily. She had been sickened by cases of abused children. ''How could you keep silent?''

He leaned back in the chair like a tired, defeated man. '''Cause I'd been protecting Varina since she was just a pretty little girl who sat behind me in the first grade. There's never been anyone but her for me. I've always looked out for her...even when Ben came along.''

''And you went on protecting her even when you suspected she might be guilty of murder?''

''I had no proof!''

''But when Jarrett showed up and I showed you the photograph, you suspected something, didn't you?

That's why you were warning Varina to watch her step, wasn't it?''

"I thought she might do something . . . foolish."

"Foolish! Like trying to kill us?" Her tone was scathing. "You could have done something to—"

Jarrett and the sheriff walked in at that moment. Griff fell silent and Jarrett looked at her with a worried expression. "Are you all right?"

She bit her lip and nodded. No use railing at Griff. She knew that for years he'd been paying for his devotion to the scheming Varina Mitchell.

The sheriff cleared his throat. "If you wouldn't mind, Miss . . ." He looked at his notebook. "Miss Delevan. Would you tell me what happened this evening . . . before Varina left the house?"

She began with dinner and Varina's speculation about Jarrett being a son of Donald Mitchell, a cousin of Benjamin's. "She left us to get the address and that's when she must have drugged the coffee." Lynne's voice was steady as she described Varina's attack on her and repeated what the crazed woman had said. She told him about the struggle for the gun.

"And she shot wildly into the wall?" He frowned. "Why did she do that?"

Lynne kept her gaze steady. "I don't know. She must have been disoriented."

"Well, I guess I've got enough for my report." He turned to Jarrett. "We'll be doing some checking, Mr. Taylor. Undoubtedly there will be some birth records that will verify your identity." His Adam's apple bobbed in his narrow throat. "I'm finding this whole yarn a bit hard to believe."

Lynne smiled wanly at him. *You don't know the half of it.*

Their bags were packed and they were ready to leave for Santa Fe when Jarrett came upstairs to get her last suitcase.

"I think I have everything," she said, glancing around.

"We'll be coming back, you know." He reached out and pulled her close. "Mr. and Mrs. Jarrett Taylor Mitchell. And we'll live happily ever after in this wonderful old house."

She looked up at him with a warm smile. *Yes, I know.*

He frowned. "It's going to take some getting used to . . . all of this."

"Oh, I don't know," she answered smugly, keeping her secret about the nursery and the double bassinets for a little boy and girl with dark hair and midnight blue eyes. She would act surprised when infant twins were placed in her arms.

The evil miasma of the house had dissipated with Varina's death. Lynne wandered through the rooms feeling secure, warm and contented. Benjamin's lingering spirit had been satisfied. She knew there was no reason for her ever to be drawn into the past again.

She looked boldly into the oval mirror as she leaned back against Jarrett. Her eyes reflected her love for him.

He bent his head and kissed the nape of her neck, trailing kisses on her tingling skin. "I love you, Lynne," he said seriously. "Love you, love you, love you," he punctuated each kiss with a caressing murmur.

She smiled happily. "And I love you."

His hands moved suggestively down her body. The hungry, lazy look in his eyes told her that they wouldn't be leaving just yet.

She smiled at her reflection in the mirror and sighed. *The future is now.*

*   *   *   *   *

And now,
an exciting preview of

THE LAST CAVALIER

by Heather Graham Pozzessere

Look for THE LAST CAVALIER and two
other
haunting Silhouette Shadows™ romances
available this month.

And every month from now on, watch for
two new Silhouette Shadows novels,
stories from the dark side of love,
wherever Silhouette books are sold.

CHAPTER ONE

Blackfield's Mountain
September, 1862
Before...

The Confederate cavalry officer stood staring down Blackfield's Mountain, his gloved hands on his hips, his silver-gray eyes fixed on the field stretching out below him. His plumed hat sat low over his brow, concealing any emotion in his eyes from his waiting men. He knew how to command, how to be stern, how to be merciful. He knew how to instill his men with courage, while also doing his damnedest to keep them all alive.

A spasm of unease suddenly crept along his spine. There was something he didn't like about the day. It was early morning; but already the battlefield was nearly black with powder from Yankee mortar and Confederate Napoleons. A man could barely see two feet in front of his face.

There seemed to be a promise of rain from the heavens above. The distant clouds, which had grown as black as the powder of cannon fire, seemed to billow and roil in a constant, wild commotion. Yet here, where he stood, the day seemed unbelievably still.

A tempest was coming. A tempest deeper than battle, louder than any clash of steel. It seemed as if God himself had grown angry with the fratricide and was about to grumble out his wrath. There was something ethereal about the air. Something tense, something charged with a strange lightning...

Something ghostly...

But Jason Tarkenton had given the order to charge, and so he would.

Today, both the Yanks and the Rebs would be forced to use their cavalry units to fight. The enemy had been gathering in the valley, preparing to attack. He would have to take the initiative.

"Charge!" Jason ordered.

"Yessir!" rose the voices of his men.

Jason's saber slashed through the air as he stretched low over his horse's neck, leading the advance.

He felt the hoofbeats pound beneath him, the vibration of the earth as over a hundred mounts followed hard behind him. Ahead of him lay the enemy in blue. Men and boys. Some would fall, and some would die. And soon, somewhere, someplace in time, mothers would cry and widows would grieve. And that was what war was: death and despair. But a man was called upon to fight it, and it was best not to dwell on the pain and horror.

Jason swore when a cannon shot exploded right in front of him and he was thrown from his horse. The air was so thick with the explosion of powder and earth that he couldn't see a damned thing. A wind had risen with the cannon shot. A strange wind. One that seemed to come from both the east and the west.

No, the wind couldn't come from the east and the west, especially not when the day had been dead calm just a few minutes ago. Dead calm, with a leaden gray sky.

But despite the strange wind, the powder swirl that had filled the air did not settle. It seemed to grow. Odd. There was a loud crack in the sky, like the sound of a cannon, but distinctly *not* the sound of a cannon.

He stared skyward. Clouds, billowing black and gray, seemed to rush down toward him. There was an arbor of large oaks just to his side. Huge trees that reached the clouds themselves, their branches forming an archway. The clouds curled back into themselves, puffing and swirling in the archway formed by the swaying branches of the trees. He realized in amazement that a strange doorway had been created in the arbor, in the blowing clouds and mist.

All around him strange winds rose, and in their whistling gust he heard a mournful wail, a cry that seemed to echo from the very heart of the dark twisting heavens. The lashing branches moved like gigantic bony arms, mocking him, beckoning him closer, into their skeletal embrace. And as he watched, an unearthly sensation swept over his body from head to toe, as if someone—or something—was touching him. Touching him with clammy fingers that trailed a chilling path down the length of his spine.

The sounds of battle grew dim, as if the fighting was taking place in the far-off distance—as if he heard no more than a memory of those sounds.

Jason couldn't see a thing. He pushed himself up from the ground and stuck his arms out into the black mist, trying to feel something ahead. He didn't have time to wait for whatever this was to blow over. He had to keep walking.

The trees! There they were ahead of him. The trees where the clouds had created a shadowy passage through the darkness and the mist. He had to reach the trees.

The wind picked up violently. He didn't need to walk toward the trees; he was being swept there.

Fingers! he thought wildly for a moment. Yes, it was as if the bony fingers of some huge, unnatural hand were reaching for him, dragging him forward. He gritted his teeth, trying with all his strength to push against the funneling winds. But those fingers had captured him in their damp, bone-chilling grip. It was like living a nightmare, feeling himself suspended in time, trapped in the twisting darkness of this unearthly tempest. The winds howled around him like the mournful voices of lost souls, their chill screams like babbling curses hanging in the air.

He was a soldier in Lee's great army of Northern Virginia! he reminded himself, shaking off the feelings. He had to be afraid of Yankee guns and sabers, and he had to rage against any strange winds that stood in his way.

Keep moving! But even as he moved, the earth seemed to shift beneath his feet. Then all of a sudden it was as if he'd walked into a brick wall. He veered back, tripped and started to roll.

"Damnation!" he muttered. Bony fingers be damned, tempests be damned, with his luck he'd roll right into a Yank troop.

The blackness swallowed him. He was a part of it now, he thought. He reached out desperately to stop himself.

His head hit a rock, and stars burst inside his mind. The trees! He had come between them; he was rolling beneath the branches that touched the skies. Now they, too, with long, bleached white, bony fingers, seemed to reach and stroke and scratch the sky.

Later he opened his eyes. For a moment, he lay still. He was still on the mountaintop; he hadn't gone very far.

And yet things were different. The blackness was gone. As if he had blinked it away. He looked up. The sky was a vivid blue, and the sun was blazing golden. He could hear a whistle, but no eerie moans, no sounds of battle.

"What the bloody hell is going on?" he muttered aloud. Had he been unconscious so long? He had thought he'd barely blacked out—just seconds.

He started to rise, but then he heard someone calling out, and he ducked down. Staring downhill through the long grasses, he could see row after row of tents. Army-issue, Union tents. Cooking fires blazed away between the tents, and delicious aromas rose from pots hanging over them. Men and women mingled.

The women were in simple cotton dresses; few seemed to be wearing petticoats. They were well dressed for army camp life. The men were in blue. Yankee-issue blue.

Jason pressed his palm against his temple. Damn, it seemed he had stumbled into the main portion of the Union army!

Quickly Jason crawled behind a large boulder and leaned back against it. He closed his eyes. How had he come here? And just where the hell *was* here?

Blackfield's Mountain
Now...

Vickie smiled sweetly at the six old men filling her grandfather's tiny tavern and reminded them, "The war ended quite some time ago, you know. Well over a hundred years ago now! It was 1865, remember?"

The men grinned sheepishly.

This was a big week for the small Virginia mining town. Not only would the battle the men were arguing about be reenacted on Saturday, but already some of the largest reenactment encampments ever drawn together were being set up in Miller's cornfield right alongside the mountain. Everyone in town was involved in the reenactment in some way.

Of course, Gramps had always been a major-league Civil War buff. And therefore, she thought, so was she. He had gleefully decided that with all the tourists in town, they should dress just like the reenactors. There sat Gramps, wearing a Virginia militia field uniform, and she was walking around serving coffee and beer in a long antebellum dress. Gramps wanted to get the folks into the spirit of the festivities when they came in for their sandwiches and drinks.

Glancing up at the clock, she saw the afternoon was gone. "Do you need me anymore, Gramps?"

"No, honey—you run on out and see your friends." He hesitated and added gruffly, "You still going to the Yankee camp?"

Vickie had to laugh, setting a kiss on his bald head. "Gramps, the war is over! And I hate to tell you this, but they did win, you know!" She heard him grunt, and she rose, winking at his comrades.

"If I were you, young lady, I'd take that little filly of yours rather than driving. They aren't letting any cars into the fields where the tents are pitched. Since they have a bunch of the historical-society types coming, they're trying to make everything look authentic."

She wasn't all that far from the encampments, and Arabesque could certainly use the exercise. She kissed her grandfather again. "'Night, Gramps."

"Don't you fraternize with them Yankees too long."

Vickie smiled, then passed from the taproom into the entryway of the house. In the dim light, she caught sight of her reflection in the wavery hallway mirror. She definitely looked the part that Gramps had asked her to play. Her simple cotton gown had a high-buttoned bodice and a small frill of lace along the wrists, neckline and hem. It was pretty, and the dark plaid went with her deep auburn hair and blue eyes.

Leaving the house, she walked around to the rear of the old barn and into the stables. Arabesque was a beautiful Arabian mare. In the deep and painful confusion that had haunted her after her husband's death, Vickie had roamed the endless blue and green fields and forests of the Virginia countryside on the sweet, spirited creature, and she'd come to know a certain peace. Now she mounted her beloved mare and rode off.

She hadn't gone very far before she realized that she'd truly left the light of civilization far behind. She was well accustomed to this country, but this night seemed exceptionally dark. There was no moon above to light her way. She reined Arabesque to a stop, suddenly seized by an eerie feeling of impending danger.

"How can I be afraid?" she mocked herself out loud. But it was dark. Awfully dark.

And no mattter what she told herself, a feeling of unease had taken root inside her. Arabesque seemed uneasy, as well. She suddenly whinnied, then reared. A night breeze picked up, strong and wild.

There was a blur in the darkness, and suddenly a figure leapt from behind a rock. A man.

Vickie shrieked in terror as Arabesque reared wildly again, pitching her over backward and then running off. She heard a mumbled intonation of fury from the man, and she tried to get up, but rough hands held her by the shoulders, then dragged her to her feet.

She knew she should be afraid. But the fear hadn't sunk in yet. She was staring at him, realizing that he was very handsome. She noticed his cavalry hat then, and the large sweeping plume that protruded from it. His uniform was gray wool with yellow trim. Southern cavalry. Authentic, right down to the dust and gunpowder marks.

His hand clamped over her mouth. She started to struggle but suddenly found herself held tightly in his arms. She felt the simmering fire of his eyes as they stared warningly down into hers.

"Sorry, ma'am. But you aren't going to get me caught!"

Caught? Wasn't he taking this playacting just a little too seriously? She twisted, kicking him in the shin. She was furious, but now panic was beginning to seize hold of her, too.

"All I wanted was your horse, but I've lost that now. I really don't mean you any harm, but I'll be damned before I'll let any Yankee-loving woman get me tossed into a prison camp for the duration of this war!"

Suddenly he bent low and butted her belly with his shoulder, throwing her over his back. The air was knocked clean from her. She gasped, desperate for breath. She couldn't scream, couldn't breathe. And he was running, with her weight bearing him down, heading for the trees that rimmed the crest of the mountain....

Welcome To The
Dark Side Of Love . . .

COMING NEXT MONTH

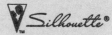